URBAN MAGIC AND OTHER TALES

CHRIS ANDREWS

CREATIVE MANUSCRIPT SERVICES

FOREWORD

Everyone loves a good Forward.

You're welcome.

URBAN MAGIC – EVERYTHING
COMES BACK

A VEIL OF GODS SHORT STORY

Everything
Comes Back

An Urban Magic Short Story

Chris Andrews

Sharon collapsed to the lounge, breathing hard. Magic, she decided, was better than sex. The spent crystal fell from her fingers to the carpet, marked with blood from where her nails had bit into her palm. Sweat stuck her hair to her left cheek and forehead.

She rested a few minutes before forcing herself to go to the bathroom to rinse her face with cold water. She pulled her damp hair back so she could see her reflection in the mirror, and squealed in delight. She looked nineteen again.

The phone rang in the other room. She closed her eyes and pressed her forehead against the cool mirror for three full rings before going out to answer it.

"Sharon here." She smiled. Even her voice sounded younger.

"Mum? Is that you? It's Georgia."

Sharon's throat closed and she almost choked. She coughed, holding the phone away. Finally, she said, "Yeah. It's me." God, her daughter's voice sounded older than her own. Years older. Time flies when you're getting younger. How old would Georgia be now? Mid-twenties? Thirty?

"Mum, I'm in town and I need to see you. I got your number from Pop but he didn't have your address."

Sharon crossed to the lounge and collapsed, running her fingers through her soft brown hair. "Uh, Georgia. I don't think seeing each other is a good idea." She glanced at the back of her hand, a young woman's hand.

She heard Georgia sniff. "Mum, I haven't seen you since I was fourteen. Fifteen years, Mum. I just want to see you. Please." She sounded like she was trying hard not to cry.

Sharon closed her eyes, resting her head against the back of the lounge. "God, I want to see you too, but-"

"Mum, please!"

She didn't respond for a moment. How could she explain? Maybe she could ask Mal to throw an illusion over her. "Fine," she said. "How about tomorrow evening?"

"Works for me."

"5pm? Where are you?"

"Unit 3, Total Comfort Motor Inn," Georgia said.

"Okay. See you there." Sharon hung up. How often had she dreamed of this moment, hoping for the call? She hadn't realised she dreaded it too.

The phone rang again and she picked it up. "Sharon here."

"What the hell are you doing?" Mal asked in his deep voice.

She felt the skin on the back of her neck prickle. "What are you talking about?"

"You just Gifted yourself with another Measure of magic. I want to know why."

Oh shit. "How the hell…? How did you know?"

"You were my apprentice. Of course I know."

That explained nothing. "So what's the problem?"

"You should have consulted me."

"There's no danger, is there? It's been a full year."

She heard him sigh. "No. I suppose not. I'm no longer your master, at any rate. I do care for you though, and I'd appreciate it if you'd seek my advice on occasion."

Was that an invitation? She jumped at the chance. "Do you have any advice now?"

"I'm glad you asked." He sounded as if he meant it. "It's well past the time when you should change your identity. You're in your late-fifties, but I'd doubt you look more than twenty-one after that last Measure."

Sharon suppressed a grin. "Younger. How about we discuss it Monday? I'm beat." She hesitated. "I do have a favour to ask though."

There was a long pause. "Monday'll do. What's the favour?"

"I've agreed to meet my daughter tomorrow night. Any chance you could throw an illusion over me beforehand?" There was a long pause, in which she could almost hear his disapproval. "It's just an illusion. Can you help me please?"

"Hmph. You wouldn't be up to a solid, moving image yet, would you?"

"No. Just minor changes to objects." Illusions were far more difficult than altering matter.

He sighed. "Fine. When do you need the illusion?"

"Tomorrow night. Afternoon, actually."

"I'll drop by around four."

"Thank you. I mean it."

There was a short silence, which told her all she needed to know about what he thought of her thanks. "See you tomorrow." He hung up.

She rested all afternoon before visiting her father that evening. Nearly blind, he hadn't noticed her getting younger over the years. When he didn't answer the doorbell she used her keys.

Sharon stopped in the entry, shocked. Books lay on the floor and photos had been knocked over. Everything that could be rifled through had been. "Oh shit." She ran for his bedroom. "Dad! Dad!"

She found him lying on his back across his bed, half his face swollen and bruised, his breathing shallow. "Dad," she whispered, grasping his dry hand. He didn't respond. "Dad?"

Her stomach did a slow roll. She dialled emergency. "Ambulance," she said breathlessly, and as prompted gave a young man the details. When she hung up she touched her father's unbruised cheek, but left him where he was. His breath rasped. She hoped he didn't have a broken rib, or worse. "The bastards," she swore. Drug addicts looking for cash, or perhaps kids setting up a new place and not wanting to pay for it. Probably both.

Anger made her want to vomit. With fresh determination she sat on the floor and focused her magical energies on the room, opening her senses to the impressions stamped there.

Sharp violence assaulted her, sickening in its uncaring malevolence. Eclipsed by the anger and hatred she felt the presence of her father, and to a lesser degree, traces of her own aura. More recently, that of her daughter, who came to visit him a few times a year. And then she noticed just one more aura. A new one. Fresh. Almost lost in the violence itself, she managed to pull the impressions the aura into a coherent representation of a person and set them in her memory.

She checked on her father. His breathing sounded no worse. "I'll get him, dad," she whispered. "Whoever it is isn't getting away with this." She sat back down and closed her eyes, taking a moment to calm herself. After a deep breath, she summoned her energies and separated her body from her soul. Having no more time than she could survive on one breath, she flew high above a world lit by life's energies. Thousands of softly glowing auras flared colourfully with ever-shifting emotions, every one more individual than a face. She searched in a quickly expanding spiral, far faster than any physical attempt could achieve.

She finally found the real-life match to the aura in her memory halfway across the town. Anger simmered deep inside her, and she wished she had the power to influence thoughts or dreams. Carefully, she bound magic into a marker she could use as a beacon, and cast it over the person's aura. She opened her eyes, angry at her impotence to do anything more.

It wasn't long before she heard an ambulance's siren and let the medics in. After they assessed her father she rode to the hospital with him, holding his hand long into the night.

She must have dozed off, because someone woke her. "What?" she asked, rubbing sleep from her eyes.

Mal crouched before her, his dark skin looking far older than it needed to be. "I've been speaking to the doctor. I hope you don't mind."

She blinked. "Is it morning? How did you know where I was?"

Sharon began to stand up, but he put a hand on her shoulder. "Take it easy. You ready to listen?"

She nodded. "It's not good, is it?"

He shook his shaved head. "He's dying, Sharon. There's nothing they can do."

Her hands pressed against her face. "Oh." That sounded lame. "Oh dear."

"You okay?" he asked. "You sound distant." His dark fingers closed around her pale ones.

"Yeah, fine," she said. A tear broke from her left eye and she violently wiped it away.

He pulled her close and held her. After a few minutes she gently pushed him away. "I must look terrible," she said. "I'm sorry." She dry-washed her face. "With all this magic, you'd think there would be something I could do." She glanced at her father, laying prone in the bed opposite her. "God, he's dying. It's hard to believe."

"Shush," he said. "It's not your fault. He's an old man. You've given him every opportunity to ask about your gifts. Considering he hasn't, I doubt he'd allow you to heal him anyway, even if you had the skill."

"You do," she suggested hopefully.

He gave her a look full of disapproval. "Not unless he asks, and certainly not without his knowledge. You know the rules"

Sharon sat down. "It's so frustrating!" she said. "I didn't think it would be this hard. I feel like an outcast in my own life."

He took her hand. There was a look on his face that said more than she wanted to hear. She glanced at her father and back, shaking her head as she held Mal's cheek with her free hand. "I know what you're going to say. Please don't. Not yet."

He turned his attention to the floor, staring for a long time before speaking. "I understand. I did the same myself." He kissed her cheek. "I'll leave you alone with him." He stood to leave, then hesitated. "Are you still meeting your daughter tonight, considering what's happened?"

Sharon blinked tears from her eyes. "I suppose," she said. "No point in putting it off."

He nodded. "I'll be there at four. Call me if anything changes."

"Thanks," she said, sniffing.

An hour after Mal left, her father's condition worsened. A few minutes later he breathed his last without waking up. She sensed his spirit leave his body.

Sharon wiped tears from her cheeks as she left the hospital, her stomach nauseous with anger. She took a seat at an empty bus stop and closed her eyes, impulsively projecting her spirit free of her body again. In seconds she found her marker, directly between her and the city centre. With no plan in mind she took the next bus heading that way.

The bus took her through centrally located, high-density public housing at the edge of the city centre. She checked her marker again. Very close. She turned to watch three kids fighting when her quarry ran out of a walkway and along the footpath, heading in the same direction as the bus. She twisted in her seat to get a good look at him. Dark hair. Skinny. Unshaven. Faded black jeans. Torn t-shirt under an old leather jacket.

The bus stopped and she stood to disembark before realising he was boarding behind three others. Heart pounding with anxiety, she dropped back into her seat as he climbed on and moved past her, down the back. She tried not to think about him as the bus left the curb, but nervous tension kept her on edge. She wanted to hurt him as badly as he had her father. Worse. She pushed aside thoughts of what Mal would say to that.

Sharon closed her eyes, letting her spiritual senses override her. His sickening addiction to heroin swept over her, nearly causing her to vomit. She swallowed bile and forced the feel of his addiction away, quickly sensing his awareness of the drug's presence in his jacket pocket. Unwilling to empathise any more, she slipped back to her natural senses.

She pictured him at her father's house - couldn't stop visualising him hitting her father and stealing whatever he could find. All to pay for his drugs. Anger and rage burned, and she blinked tears. After a while cold fury settled deep in her chest. She stared out the window with tears on her cheeks, barely aware her hands had curled into fists.

He got off at the city interchange and walked down to the far end to wait for another bus. She followed him, clenching and unclenching her hands, losing the fight with her anger and hatred. Mal would have something to say about what she was about to do, but she couldn't stop herself.

Her legs shook as she stopped beside him. Her whole body trembled with the need to do something just as bad to him as he'd done to her father. Her fingers subtly brushed his jacket directly over the inside pocket. The touch was all she needed. She felt her limited senses awaken as she silently asked a Permission. By the time her fingers left the leather jacket the heroin was pure.

Relief as powerful as her anger overwhelmed her. "Everything comes back," she whispered.

He turned. "Say what?" His breath stank. His two front teeth were broken and dead.

Sharon glared. "Everything comes back," she whispered. "Many times over."

He frowned. "What the hell are you talking about kid?"

The word 'kid' almost struck her like a blow. She stumbled back and turned away, walking fast.

"Dumb slut!" he called after her.

Sharon walked to the mall near the bus interchange and wondered aimlessly around for hours, wishing she could be there when the bastard overdosed on his heroin. When she finally made her way home, Mal was waiting.

"I've been calling for hours. Where have you been?" he asked. He looked concerned.

Sharon shrugged. "Wondering aimlessly. Sorry." She unlocked her door and they went in.

It was after four. "Oh shit. I forgot about Georgia. Can you do the illusion now please? I'm going to be late."

"You sure you're up to this?" Mal asked.

No. "Yeah. I'll be fine."

She felt nothing as Mal placed the illusion on her. Looking in the mirror she seemed to have aged nearly forty years. She wasn't sure what to say. "Am I glad I met you. I don't ever want to look like that." Even her voice sounded old.

Mal laughed, deep and strong. "The joys of magic, huh? You want a lift?"

Sharon smiled. "Yeah, that'd be great. Thanks."

They arrived at the motel just before five. "Can you wait a few minutes? Just in case it doesn't go well?"

"Sure thing."

She checked the illusion in the rear-view mirror again, then got out and made her way past reception. She found her daughter's room quickly enough, but there was no answer to her knock. She tried again, then once more. "Georgia? You there?" Silence.

She closed her eyes and let her senses expand, feeling for the impressions an aura makes. She sensed pain, suffering. "Oh God, no!" she whispered.

Her senses flared as she touched the door handle. She felt the lock click and she shoved the door open, rushing inside. The stench of vomit filled her lungs. She swallowed hard, trying not to gag. The room was small, the bed to the left and the bathroom at the far end.

She made her way past the bed, then stopped in shock. Her father's murderer lay against the wall on the far side, dead, eyes staring at nothing. A deep chill washed over her.

A syringe rested on the carpet just past his outstretched hand, a tourniquet around his arm. The bed-sheets were half-pulled over him as if he'd struggled at some point.

Sharon looked away, her stomach tight with fear. She walked around the bed and the dead man. The bathroom door was slightly ajar. Her hand shaking, she rested her cheek against the doorframe. "Please don't let Georgia be in there." She slowly pushed it open.

Her daughter lay on the cold tiles, her eyes closed, but her body unmoving. Lifeless. Her bare arms were marked from the needles she'd used so often - her flesh wasted and abused. Sharon's eyes blurred and she wanted to be sick. She turned and ran from the room, vomiting violently against a tree. She wiped her mouth with the back of her hand, stumbling, half blind with tears. She made it back to Mal's car, weeping uncontrollably.

"She's dead, Mal. Oh God. She's dead." She crumpled into the passenger seat. Mal passed her a hanky and placed a comforting arm across her shoulders. She wiped her eyes and lips, then cleaned the vomit from the back of her hand. Crying overcame her again, huge sobs she couldn't control. Mal held her until the tears eased and she finally pulled away.

"Another?" he asked, holding a fresh hanky out.

She took it, wiping her eyes again. "Why did this have to happen?"

When he didn't respond, she turned and found him watching her. A cold feeling momentarily overwhelmed her grief. "You know what I did!"

There was no judgement in his eyes, only compassion. "No. How could I? I sensed it through your emotions."

"Oh Mal. Why didn't you stop me?"

Sharon began to cry again. He pulled her close and waited it out. When she finally stopped, he said, "Even if I'd been there to advise you, I couldn't have foreseen the consequences any more than you could."

"I never imagined this. I could have lived with his death. Not my daughter's."

There was a long silence. "It gets worse," Mal said.

She looked up at him, eyes red and teary. "Nothing could make it any worse."

He frowned, but not in anger. She saw only a deep sadness and regret. He glanced down as he spoke. "It's time to change your identity." He glanced at the hotel, at the door of the room she'd just vacated. "Georgia."

Afterward

The Urban Magic short stories in this collection came about for a couple of reasons.

The main reason was about exploring how magic fits into human society unnoticed. I didn't want to change the world, just add a hidden layer to it, so it had to be subtle.

Having a secret society of people who'd found a way to expand their perceptions and alter reality around them worked, and Everything Comes Back was one of my first forays into this world.

The only real rule I made was that it had to fit into the Veil of Gods story universe, of which most of my novels are (or will) be a part.

A VEIL OF GODS SHORT STORY

indy braked hard, forcing Henry to brace a hand against the dash. "Go easy. You haven't paid for it yet."

"Mermaids," Mindy whispered as she stared through a gap in the rainforest to the nearby bay.

Just visible through broad tropical leaves and the drooping roots of a strangler fig, three girls were splashing about in a wide cove, throwing a volleyball to each other.

"Tourists," Henry muttered. Stinger season was done, but crocs didn't have a season. "We've got to get them out of the water."

"Can't you see their tails?" Mindy stared at him as if he were crazy.

He glanced at the dark bruise on her forehead. "Perhaps you shouldn't be driving." She'd called this morning to accept his offer to buy the ute, but only if he let her test its four-wheel-drive capabilities during an overnight camping trip, for 'old time's sake'. Mindy put the ute in gear and followed the sandy path to the cove, getting out the moment they arrived. Henry followed her onto the hot sand, the sun harsh on his balding head.

Toned to the point of being cut, the girls were waist-deep in the water. They looked like they spent enough time outdoors to know better than to swim this far north.

"You all need to clear out of the water," Henry called. "There's crocs up here."

"It's hot," the redhead said as the volleyball splashed near her, thrown by the brunette.

"I've swam with 'gaters before," said the blonde in an American accent. "They ain't so bad."

"Crocs aren't alligators!"

The redhead watched Mindy with interest. "Why are you two here?"

"The old bastard's trying to flog off his ute."

Old bastard? Henry gave her look. He wanted to see his twin grandsons who'd just started crawling, but he needed money to fly across the country. Time was running out. "Are you girls lost?" he asked. "I don't see any camping gear." Certainly no car or boat.

"Can you spare a beer?" the redhead asked Mindy with an inviting smile. "It's been a while."

"Strawberry..." the shortest of the three began with a warning in her tone. She'd braided her dark hair at the sides and blended the two braids behind her head, the rest cascading down her back to the water.

Mindy returned the smile. "Anything for a redhead." She pushed her own dyed locks from her face, exposing the dark bruise once more.

Strawberry squealed and waded from the water, linking arms with Mindy to walk with her to the ute. The blonde sighed with a long-suffering glance at the other girl and trailed after them, kicking at dry sand as she stomped up the beach.

Mindy batted for both teams? How the hell didn't he know that? "We don't bite," Henry said to the brunette, almost as an afterthought. She hadn't moved from the water.

She smiled as if he'd just made a joke. "You don't recognise me, do you?" She stared almost as invitingly as Strawberry had smiled at Mindy.

What would such a gorgeous young girl want with an old man like him? He shifted his feet uncomfortably. "Should I?"

Her eyes betrayed disappointment. "When did you hook up with her?"

He shrugged. "We went out a few times, but never really hit it off. Please come out of the water. It really is dangerous."

She sighed and did as he asked, stopping as she reached him. "You're dying," she said softly, reaching out to place a gentle palm against his cheek. The familiarity was disconcerting. "Aren't you? My father had the same smell before he died."

Surprised, he nodded. "Cancer. As soon as I get enough money I'm going to visit my son and grandkids."

That produced a smile. "You made a life for yourself. I'm glad." She held out her hand. "Carmen."

Her name sounded familiar, particularly the way she said it. "Henry." He shook and they walked back to the trees.

Carmen pointed to the redhead. "That's Linda. We call her Strawberry Shortcake because she hates it. The blonde's Miriam Tinker. Tinkerbell, or Tink for short. She hates that too. They call me Queen Cow."

"Do you hate your nickname as well?"

She smiled. "Someone I loved used to call me Angel. Nobody's dared call me that since." She watched his eyes as if expecting a reaction, but it only made him uncomfortable.

Mindy walked up to the two of them, holding a can of beer. "Henry and I have business, Carmen. Hands off."

"Sure, if you stay away from my sister."

Carmen and Strawberry looked nothing alike.

Mindy raised her chin as if she'd just been given a challenge. "Hey Strawberry, how about you and me go halves in a religious experience?"

Strawberry glanced at Carmen with just a hint of indecision. Carmen gave her a slight shake of her head, which seemed to give Strawberry all the resolve she needed. "You think you're up to a religious experience?" she asked.

"Test me out," Mindy said, eyes challenging Carmen the whole time.

Henry glanced from one girl to another until Strawberry linked arms with Mindy and they wondered off along the beach, disappearing into the trees. What the hell was going on?

"Want me to drown the minx?" Tink asked Carmen. Carmen gave her a look.

"Did you girls hike in?" Henry asked to break the tense silence which followed. "I don't see any gear."

"We swam in," Tink said with sarcasm. "Care to come for a swim with me?"

"Tink, please. You know this isn't easy for me," Carmen said before giving Henry a sidelong glance. "Our campsite's up on the headland Henry, safe from crocs."

"Whatever," Tink said, slouching. "Mindy rem..." She glanced at

Henry with a frown. She rubbed her forehead in the place where Mindy had the bruise, a question in her eyes. Carmen nodded.

Henry felt like he'd been ambushed. Or betrayed. Or... something. "Mindy was hoping to meet Strawberry here, wasn't she?" Had she ever intended to buy his ute?

"Appears that way," Carmen said.

"We should get a fire going. It's getting late." Henry found a rock-lined fire pit on the edge of the trees, and plenty of driftwood and kindling nearby. He built the fire while Carmen strode the beach like she had the title stashed in her bikini, watching for Strawberry and Mindy the entire time.

Both Carmen and Tink refused anything to eat, but downed a couple of beers in the hour before Mindy came back holding hands with Strawberry. Blue and green flames from the salt in the driftwood illuminated their approach.

"Who's up for a bourbon?" Henry asked.

"I'll have one with you," Carmen said with a smile that seemed too familiar, following him to the ute.

Pulling the tailgate down, he used it as a bench to pour two drinks over ice from the esky. Carmen held hers up with a smile before throwing it back. He took a sip.

"What's the matter?" she glanced at his drink with a raised eyebrow.

"Too old to drink hard."

She moved a little too close. "Do me a favour?"

"Another drink?"

"Leave. Tonight. Strawberry had a thing for Mindy a while ago, but it's over, or at least it needs to be. I'll make it up to you if you can convince her to go."

"I'm not her father." Besides, he needed her money for the ute, though he figured the chances of that materialising after tonight's camping trip were thin to none.

Carmen rested a suggestive hand on his chest. "I'll *really* make it worth your time."

He was almost old enough be her grandfather. Henry stepped back and gently removed her hand. "Perhaps you should let Strawberry and Mindy sort out their differences on their own."

Carmen gave him a look his ex-wife would have been impressed with and stomped away. Henry sighed, downed his drink and poured another as Mindy walked up.

"That mine?" she asked, taking his drink from his hand and downing it. She slapped the glass on the tailgate and pulled two beers from the esky, ice clattering to the metal.

"Feeling a little used, to be honest." He gave her a flat stare.

Mindy leaned her hip against the rusty tailgate, returning the look. "You dumped me for some whore in a bar. What do you care?"

"A month after you told me to get the hell out and never return."

She kept eye contact, but only just. "Carmen looks… irritated. You can't do anything right, can you?"

He wasn't going to be drawn into another fight. "We should set up for the night."

When they returned to the fire with their rolled-up swags, Henry just sat on his. "Maybe you girls should head back to your campsite before it gets too dark. You'll need to get a fire going if you want to cook dinner."

Mindy put her hand on Strawberry's knee and slid it up her inner thigh. "Some of us have plans that don't involve cooking."

Carmen glared at Henry from across the flames, her features illuminated by flickering firelight.

"What?" he asked.

She stood and walked into the gloom.

"When did you two get married?" Mindy asked loudly enough to ensure Carmen heard.

"I was thinking the same thing," Henry whispered as he watched the flames.

Three drinks later and a lot of awkward silence, Henry put his empty glass on a tree root. "I'm crashing."

"Die in your swag and I'm leaving you for the crocs," Mindy said, making Strawberry laugh. Tink studied her sandy toes.

Henry unrolled his swag, brushed off his sandy feet and crawled in on top of his sleeping bag. What he wouldn't give to be three-thousand kilometres away on a Perth beach meeting his grandkids for the first time.

* * *

It felt like he'd barely fallen asleep when a shotgun blast woke him. Henry shoved the canvass back and sat bolt upright, heart pounding as startled fruit bats filled the night sky. The campfire had died to coals. Mindy and the girls were gone. Except for the sounds of startled fruit bats and lapping waves, everything returned to quiet.

Heart still thumping, Henry slipped quietly out of his swag and made for the ute, hoping the girls were there already. The ute was gone. "Oh for..." It had to be a good fifteen kilometres over rough terrain back to the main road. He couldn't suppress a wave and fear at being abandoned with a shooter in the region.

A woman cleared her throat. Henry spun. Carmen stood a few metres away, the darkness hiding her expression. "Mindy said she'll kill Strawberry and Tink if you don't go to her."

"What?" He couldn't hide his disbelief.

Carmen took an angry step toward him, fists clenched at her side. "She took my sisters."

He held his hands up, palms outward. "Calm down. What happened?"

"Help me save my sisters and you can have anything within my power. I promise. Just name it."

"I'd like to live long enough to see my grandchildren grow up. Can you do that?" he asked with enough sarcasm to make anyone but Carmen flinch. Her frown deepened into a glare. "What's going on Carmen? Really?"

"Come with me." She strode past him, walking along the beach. When he didn't follow, she glanced over her shoulder, her features softening. "Please."

With few other options, he followed. They found Mindy sitting on a rock close to the water, a shotgun pointed at Tink who stood on the sand.

"Why are you doing this Mindy?" Henry asked with more than a little nervousness. How had she got the shotgun into his ute without him seeing it?

Mindy swung the gun on Henry and then back at Tink. "They can have Strawberry when they give me what I want."

"And what's that?"

"They're mermaids, and I want to be one of them." She wasn't just delirious from the bruise on her head. She was insane.

"Go stand in the water," Mindy said to him. When he hesitated she turned the weapon on him. "Now!"

Henry raised his hands. "Aren't we friends?"

"Of course not. You're just the bastard who lied about how much he loved me. Stand in the water. Now."

"Please do as she says," Carmen said.

Beginning to fear for his life, Henry walked until water washed around his ankles. Mindy's shotgun followed him the whole way. If there was a croc nearby...

"You," Mindy said to Tink. "Promise you'll stay out of this. I know you can't break a promise."

"No."

"You want Strawberry dead?" Mindy raised the shotgun to make the threat clear.

"Mindy," Henry began. "Mermaids aren't real."

She stared at him as if he were an idiot. "I forgot everything until I hit my head, but I remember now. I met Strawberry when I was fifteen. Fifteen! She hasn't aged in twenty-nine years! I want to be young again. If I can't have that, they can't have Strawberry back."

"We can fix this without the gun..."

Mindy aimed the shotgun at Tink again. "Make the promise! I've got silver pellets in here. I know they'll kill you."

"Do it Tink," Carmen said. "I'll make the deal for Strawberry."

Tink gave Carmen a long look, but finally nodded. "I promise not to interfere, but if Strawberry's not returned safely I also promise to hunt you down and give you the most horrible death I can think of."

Carmen took a cautious step forward. "Strawberry loves you Mindy. Isn't that enough?"

"No. She could have changed me, but she let me to grow old instead. Why?"

"You know why," Carmen said with an oddly tender glance at Henry. "It's better this way. Go live your life like you were supposed to. Forget Strawberry. I did the same for Henry a long time ago."

A cold shiver passed through Henry, complete with a flash of barely recalled memory. "You and me..." he whispered. "Were we lovers when I was young?"

Mindy pointed a finger at Henry. "Use him to transform me. He's dying anyway."

"I'll do what you ask," Carmen said to Mindy. "But you have to return Strawberry first. I won't risk it otherwise."

"Change me first and I'll tell you where she is afterward."

"Not until she's released."

Mindy bit her bottom lip. "Make me a promise then. I know you can't break a promise. Swear you'll turn me into a mermaid if I tell you where Strawberry is."

Carmen kept her glare for a moment longer, but finally nodded. "I promise to turn you into a mermaid so long as you release Strawberry first."

"Tonight?"

"Tonight."

"Why do you need me?" Henry asked.

Carmen answered. "It takes a person's lifeforce to transform a human into one of our kind." She gave Henry a sad smile. "I told you that when we were lovers, only you can't remember."

Mindy threw the car keys to Tink. "Strawberry's in a trunk on the back of the ute on the headland. It should only take about twenty minutes to jog there."

"Go," Carmen said to Tink, who set off.

Carmen approached Henry. "I'll make it painless," she said. "You won't even know you're drowning."

"I'm not ready to die," he whispered. Not until he'd seen his grandkids.

"I'm sorry, but mermaids are bound to each other, and we can't break promises. I have to save Strawberry."

Mindy approached with the shotgun on Carmen.

Water rose and lifted Henry off his feet. He cried out as it carried him toward deep water. Carmen towed Mindy out, the shotgun still in Mindy's hand. There was clearly little trust between them.

"Carmen, please," Henry begged.

"I made a promise. The deal's struck. I no longer have a choice."

"Hurry up!" Mindy said. "Do it now. Henry's going to do one good thing for me before he dies."

Below the surface something brushed his feet and he jerked, something completely wrong. Carmen's tail. She reached for him with sharp-clawed fingertips that had been normal fingers just a minute beforehand.

"Wait, Carmen. Please!"

"I can't break a promise Henry. I know this isn't what you asked for, but it's all I can offer," Carmen said, pulling him close.

"I don't want to die," he whispered.

"Of course you don't." There was something in her expression as she kissed him, her wet, salty lips tender and soft on his. Calmness washed over him, and for a moment he didn't fight. The kiss quickly became a tingling sensation spreading through his entire body.

"You did as I asked," Carmen said. "You helped me save Strawberry and Tink. Now I have to keep my promise."

Carmen spun and ripped the shotgun from Mindy's hand, throwing it across the water with a splash.

"Hey!"

"You're going to let me go?" Henry asked with sudden hope and relief.

"No."

The fear returned, only worse. She really was going to drown him.

"Change me now!" Mindy said. "You promised."

Carmen smiled at Henry. "What was it you asked for?"

It took him a moment to follow her thoughts. "To watch my grandkids grow up," he whispered.

She smiled.

"No," he said. Carmen had reversed the play on Mindy. "Carmen, please don't do this. Just let me go."

Mindy gripped Carmen's wrist, trying to break the mermaid's hold. "No. *I* deserve to be one of you, not some dying alcoholic," Mindy said. "You promised me!"

Carmen snarled, revealing canines a croc would be intimidated by. "I promised Henry first."

"Please don't Carmen!" Henry said. The tingling sensation was growing stronger.

Carmen grabbed Mindy by the throat, sharp claws biting into her skin. Mindy screamed, the sound cutting off as Carmen forced her under the surface. Mindy struggled, her hands splashing above the surface as she tried to fight the mermaid off.

In almost as much of a panic, Henry grasped Carmen's wrist, hoping to break her hold and bring Mindy back above the surface, but Carmen was far stronger than he was. It was like gripping a metal bar.

"I'm sorry I missed your life, Henry. I really am," Carmen said. Her hand snaked behind his head and pulled him close. "But leaving you was the right thing to do, so please forgive me for that, if not what I'm about to do. I really have no choice."

"I want to see my grandkids, but not like this."

"Some things can't be fixed, Henry. I'm truly sorry."

"I'm begging you Carmen." He tried to lean away, but she held him close.

She kissed him once more, and this time it was just a kiss, tender and loving. "I'd rather live with your enmity than Mindy's spite. Please forgive me. You'll get to watch your grandchildren grow up and grow old, and have children and grandchildren of their own. I'll be with you the entire time if that's what you want, or leave you alone forever."

To watch his family grow up, even from afar... As Mindy's struggles grew weaker he couldn't avoid the words. "Then there's nothing to forgive, Carmen."

She kissed him once more as she took him beneath the surface.

Afterward

Promises Promises went through quite a few changes before its current form.

The earliest concepts revolved around the mermaids coming to shore and trying to lure men and women to a watery death (and things going wrong, of course). I didn't want the mermaids to be the antagonists though, and I didn't want them to be the victims either, so the scenario didn't really work for me.

In the first draft of the current version, Mindy kidnapped Henry to use him as a sacrifice and become a mermaid herself, but it wasn's much more than a trite horror story without any real impact, and the characters weren't developed enough to really make it work.

The second-last full draft saw Mindy as Henry's estranged and rather messed-up daughter. In that version, Henry was a very bad father who had left Mindy to fend for herself from a young age. This gave her a strong motivation to want payback. It was a stronger story, but still more of a revenge story than what I wanted.

To get it to where it is today I gave Henry and Mindy the kind of old relationship where two people get together for all the wrong reasons - hooking up with someone as badly damaged as they them-selves are so they can feel good for a little while. Their shared history with the mermaids is what damaged them in the first place, making the story into a tragedy, which worked much better than a revenge story.

Although both Henry and Mindy are damaged people, the main difference between them is that Mindy makes the wrong choices, and so becomes the antagonist.

CAPTAIN BHURATI'S LAST VOYAGE

A VEIL OF GODS SHORT STORY

Captain Bhurati squinted at the reflection of the sun on the waves, a sickly feeling in his stomach as he turned to examine his wake. He put his spyglass to his eye to check the distant rocky beach again. The wind was filling his ship's sails, but his ship wasn't moving. Despite the cool breeze, perspiration began to bead on his brow.

Fighting fear, he put his spyglass to his eye and scanned the beach once more as if doing so would change what he knew. He hoped, regardless. The small ruined cottage set within the trees which he'd been using as an indicator of movement, remained mostly hidden between two huge silver oaks, yet their position relative to each other hadn't changed. Or more accurately, his ship remained fixed in relation to the ruin and the trees. If they moved as much as a ship's length he wouldn't be able to see the ruin's left wall, yet it remained visible.

Dread crept deeper into his stomach as he considered his wife and crew, and what might happen to them. "Mercy, please Goddess," he whispered, wondering what he might have done to have offended Her.

Underneath him, his ship rocked to the rush of the Temern Straight coming out from the Sea of Lost Souls, or the Bay of Blood depending on who you spoke to. Even the wind had no effect on their position. They might as well have ran aground.

"This evening," his wife said with a smile, her boots soft on the deck as she came to stand beside him at the helm. "I'm looking forward to a golden wine and a meal that's freshly picked. We're down to hard tack as of this morning." Her body moved with the ship as it crested a mild wave and the bow dropped a foot or two.

How was he going to tell her all their lives were likely forfeit?

She squinted at the headland a mile ahead, the huge statue of the Divine Lady Cinora du Lons, Goddess of Water, rising above the trees to overlook the ocean. The statue's palms faced outward in benevolence. At night, the fires lit in her eyes guided sailors away from the rocks.

"We haven't moved much. Is the current that strong?" Dhenora asked, glancing with a frown at the water to starboard. In an hour or so the tide would bottom out, and shortly after that it would begin rushing back into the Sea of Lost Souls, but if he was right his ship wouldn't follow the water's lead or even be influenced by the wind.

He called to his first mate. "Rojan, get every inch of sail up and catching the wind. The current's too strong."

The man nodded and began giving orders to the crew.

Bhurati glanced at the shore once more, but resisted the urge to put his spyglass to his eye once more. He silently prayed for some change he suspected would never come without sacrifice to the Goddess.

How had he inadvertently insulted Her? He'd offered Her tribute before sailing.

He took a deep breath and fought his tension, dredging up the courage to confide. "You haven't been on deck for a while, love. We've been level with the shore for too long, despite the wind and tide."

He let his eyes drift to hers, saw her dark sun-kissed skin pale a little and the lines around her mouth and eyes tighten. "Ye say we're being held in place?" his wife and Trade Mistress asked. While he captained the ship, she did the important bartering when in port, and without her he'd have been done out of a lot of good coin.

Reluctantly, he nodded, his stomach in knots again, worse now after seeing his wife's fears mirroring his own. Her salt and pepper dreadlocks moved down her back, more salt near her scalp, as she shook her head in denial. Like him, her expression suggested that, as if by sheer will, she could put all to rights.

"Ye paid tribute?" she reluctantly asked, though she knew the answer before he replied.

"Aye. If the Goddess is unhappy with us, what else could it be? The wind's strong at our back and we should be cutting through the water despite the outgoing tide." When she didn't respond, he put a hand on her shoulder to calm her fears. "Whatever insult we inadvertently made, we'll sacrifice whatever extra tribute she demands and be done with it. We'll be safe, I promise."

Dhenora took a long, deep breath and seemed to hold it for too long. "Safe?" she asked in a near explosion. She took another breath, and then another. "What of our crew? The Goddess shouldn't be so cruel to us," she whispered. "Not since she took our daughter."

He turned away, not willing to remember the storm that had washed Maelayen overboard and pushed them near a hundred miles off course. Maelayen had been an even better trader than her mother.

He glanced at his sailors, good men and women who'd sailed with him for years. Family, some of them by blood. At least three were cousins. No, four of them on this voyage. Had one of his people insulted the Goddess? Other than the tribute paid before they'd left harbour, and with his ship's beautifully-carved and painted mermaid for its figurehead to honour the Goddess and daughters as well, what more could he offer? Had Her priests declared a new decree he hadn't heard?

"Could one of our competitors have begged the Goddess for a favour?" Dhenora asked. "Perhaps they seek to delay us, or worse?"

"Would the Goddess accept such unworthy offerings?" Bhurati asked, trying not to glance at the distant shore again as if that might provide him with the answer.

He checked the rigging instead, and caught Ganzan's eye. The sailor's eyes narrowed and his lips pursed. He'd noticed they weren't moving too. If one sailor had, they all would have, most likely. He gave the man a nod, letting him know that whatever the Goddess demanded in compensation or tribute, he, as Captain, would pay it. Ganzan nodded back, satisfied.

"The current runs against us. Perhaps bad luck?" Dhenora said hopefully, but he could hear the false note in her tone. She knew better. She'd lived aboard ships her whole life, just as he had, and she knew the winds and currents in the Temern Straight. This wasn't natural.

"Captain," Henniya called from the fore where she was splicing ropes, her body stiff with tension.

He followed her gaze and his fears found a fresh storm of anxiety. A mermaid bobbed in the water fifty yards off the bow, watching his ship. She had long honey-coloured hair that was almost as pale as her skin, spread out in the water behind her. Anger marred her expression. Another mermaid surfaced beside her, her skin darker than night, and her long straight hair like coal. Both of the mermaid's eyes drifted to the ship's figurehead. Without another sign, they sank below the water.

Bhurati tried to keep his shoulders straight as he glanced at the prow, glad he was holding the ship's wheel for fear his shaking hands may give his fears away. Nobody insulted mermaids. It was the one rule every sailor followed, no matter where they were from.

The ship's figurehead was the problem then. What had happened? Had the last storm damaged her and he'd failed to notice? Perhaps a piece of jetsam or flotsam had smashed into the carving on their last passage.

He glanced at the deep blue water again, but there was nothing to suggest anything amiss or mermaids were watching from below.

What did he have then? Time. The mermaids were giving him time to put things right. But how much?

"Henniya! Check the figurehead," he called to the woman splicing rope. She touched two fingers to her temple and stood, clambering onto the bowsprit and leaning over, her right hand entwined in ropes to ensure she didn't fall.

Even from the helm he could see her stiffen. She clambered down, touching her nose with a finger. The figurehead's face was damaged then. It did nothing but fill him with dread for the safety of his ship and crew.

He had to make amends, and fast. What did he have in the hold? Fruit for the markets in Haramanth, the Imperial City's largest trade square. "We have to offer them a sacrifice," he said to Dhenora. "Have the crew empty a barrel of apples over the side. Fully ripe ones. The brightest red we carry."

If only they had bolts of silk or some gold. Fruits, wines, pottery and grains made up his entire cargo this trip, and he had little coin until he could sell his merchandise. "A case of wine, too." Spilled grain would be useless to mermaids, and they wouldn't want pottery, but apples and wine they might enjoy. It might be enough.

Within minutes a barrel's worth of apples bobbed in the fast-moving current, quickly disappearing beyond the stern. Untouched. The case of wine disappeared with a splash.

"Now what?" Dhenora asked, shaking her head slightly. The apples continued to disappear, still on the surface.

"They release us and we put into the next cove, drop anchor, and fix the figurehead before sailing on."

Tense minutes passed, and then more. His crew began loitering, watching the waves. The sails, still full, did nothing to move them forward. He didn't have the courage or heart to tell his sailors to get back to work.

"If they keep us here for too long, our cargo of fruit will go rotten," Dhenora said.

"The cargo's not the issue. This will be resolved long before it spoils."

In a short time, a small fleet of three merchant ships sailed past them with the current, tacking against the wind. None offered help, and rightly so, though the pale-skinned captain of the third ship doffed his tricorn hat in solidarity upon realising their predicament. If he'd tried to help though, he'd likely draw the mermaids' enmity too.

"The mermaids can't touch our ship as long as we have the figure-head, damaged or not," Dhenora said. "They're trying to scare us."

"And succeeding," Bhurati said with a wary glance at his loitering crew. "The ship itself is protected by the Covenant, but as we've insulted them they can keep us here 'til we starve."

"What more can we sacrifice to them?" Dhenora asked. "I'll check the hold."

He squeezed her shoulder, knowing what the mermaids wanted, and knowing who had to pay it. "Someone has to go over the side to appease them for the insult." His crew would soon be looking to him to make that sacrifice, and if he didn't jump, they'd likely throw him over, family or not. Dhenora too.

Dhenora gripped his hand where it rested on his shoulder, her hands almost as calloused as his own. "You owe them nothing," she said. "This is not your fault." There was a sound of desperation in her voice now.

He met her eyes, seeing the inevitability there. She knew just as well as he did what it was going to take to see his ship free again. "I'm Captain. Whose responsibility is it if not mine?" Wishing he could think of another way, he stripped off the dagger at his belt and pulled off his boots. Dhenora could sell the rest of his gear when she arrived in port. He pulled a small silver flask from his britches and took a long swig of rum before handing what was left to her. It was likely to be his last swig, and would help with the courage needed.

She took a swig herself, but then shook her head. "No," she whispered. "Don't. The mermaids can complain to the Goddess for all I care. I'm not losing you too."

Judging by the uncompromising glances from his crew he didn't have a choice. None of them wanted to go under with him. He nodded to them, telling his crew all they needed to know. As one, they raised two fingers to their temples in respect.

"Bhurati-" Dhenora began, but he cut her off.

"It has to be," he said softly, thinking of the life now denied him. His life with her and their two sons who'd been fostered to other ships.

Barefoot, he walked to the stern, and before he could let fear talk him out of it, he gripped the handrail and vaulted overboard. Dhenora screamed as he fell.

The shock of cool water drove his fears home, but rather than the clawed hands he expected to drag him deeper, he surfaced, splashing about as the current took him away from his ship. The waters around him suddenly stilled, keeping him a dozen yards from the stern.

Something touched his leg and he cried out, a deep, manly sound, he chose to believe.

A clawed hand burst through the surface and cold fingers caught his neck. Despite his resolve to sacrifice himself, he fought anyway, gripping the wrist and trying to free himself as a beautiful red-headed woman's face emerged from the calm water, her long hair caught in the current a foot from them. She had no trouble holding him, even lifting him a foot out of the water.

She smiled wickedly, showing canines sharp enough to frighten off a shark.

"It's not you we want, Captain," she said, her voice raspy and her blue eyes narrow. "But thank you for offering. Send us the one who defaced the figurehead and we'll allow your ship to sail unharmed to Imperial City, where you can make repairs to the figurehead. Defy us and we'll keep your ship here until slavers pass, and watch as they take you all."

He croaked out a sound of assent, still struggling to pull the creature's hand away from his neck. She released him and he dropped below the surface. He splashed back up, but barely caught his breath before water tumbled him end over end. His lungs burned for the oxygen he desperately needed before he slammed into something hard. Water seemed to explode all around him, dissipating across the deck of his own ship.

Air. Fresh air. He coughed until he had nothing left but the taste of salt in his mouth. Sodden, the deck as wet as he was, it wasn't until his wife spoke that he looked up.

"What did she say?" Dhenora asked, her face lined with fear and worry as she crouched before him, her hair and clothes as soaked as he was. She caught his cheeks in her warm hands, guiding his eyes to hers.

He wiped his mouth with the back of his hand. "They want whoever defaced the figurehead. They didn't say who, but knew it wasn't me. They must have seen it happen. If we don't toss 'em overboard, they'll keep us here until slavers take us." Or they starved to death, he guessed. He doubted even slavers would dare come near a ship caught as his was.

She stiffened, shaking her head slightly in denial while his sodden crew began murmuring, questions and accusations on their lips, looking at each other as if each were an enemy. If he didn't do something soon they'd start tossing each other overboard.

"You're not telling me something," he said softly to Dhenora. "I can see it in your face. Did you see who did it? You couldn't have been so stupid as to..." He finally noticed the dread in her eyes. Genuine fear. He shook his head in denial. "You did it, didn't you?

She glanced at the sailors and he followed her gaze. They'd heard. There was abrupt fury in more than one expression as the word spread.

"You nearly killed us all," Henniya said.

If the mermaids weren't generous enough to forgive the insult, they'd all be worse than dead soon.

"We don't know who did it," she said in protest, but Bhurati knew. They all did. She could barter with the best merchants he'd ever seen, but she'd never been able to lie to him.

"Why?" Bhurati asked.

"Don't accuse me of this," she hissed, her legendary fury turning on him. "How can you say I insulted the Goddess when it was the Goddess who swept our daughter overboard?" She clapped a hand over her mouth like a child who'd just realised what she'd said. She stood and backed a step toward the stern, and then another, as the sailors formed a ring around her, trapping her against the rail.

"No," she said. "No. The Goddess deserved the insult for what she did!"

Bhurati got to his feet, pushing through his sailors to face his wife. It wouldn't take much for a superstitious lot like his crew to toss both her and him overboard if he didn't act.

The beautiful rocky beach stretched nearly a mile between the two headlands, partly cleared to the shore by farmers, but there'd be no way Dhenora could make it to shore in this current. Even if she could, the mermaids wouldn't allow it. If Dhenora went overboard they'd drown her just as sure as she'd drown if she went over in a storm.

But if she didn't go over, they'd all die. His crew, his family, would never let that happen. "You watched me give up my life for your petty revenge," he said. Steeling his heart, he found he had no voice to give the order to have her upended and thrown over the stern. Mermaids, while benign as long as you respected them, were always unforgiving, yet he couldn't do it even then.

"We could anchor off the beach and fix the figurehead ourselves," Dhenora pleaded, desperation on her face. "Gaenson isn't bad with a whittling knife. If the mermaids see us doing right by them, they might forgive us."

"Us?" Henniya asked, the crew's anger rising now. "You," she said, her tone uncompromising. The other sailors began echoing the sentiments, venting their anger. It wouldn't be long before their words turned to blades.

Bhurati raised a single hand, quieting them as he found his voice, now fuelled by his own anger at what she'd done. "You let me throw myself overboard on your behalf, and never said a word."

"But-"

He closed his fists until they hurt. "They're not here to forgive *us!*" He couldn't keep the fury from his voice, or the heartbreak. "They want you," he whispered, the final word carrying enough emotion to make his voice break.

She glanced at the uncompromising faces of the sailors, tears on her cheeks now. "They might allow it," she said. "If you just let me..." Her voice trailed off. "Please."

He'd been sailing these waters for nearly three decades, and only once seen mermaids drag a ship entirely under, taking the crew one at a time as they floundered. None sailed the oceans without a mermaid as a figurehead, not even kings and emperors. And no one insulted them by damaging their figurehead.

"You'll kill us all if you stay," he whispered. He moved forward and folded her in his arms, tears of his own falling into her dreadlocks as he held her close. It was all the comfort he could offer.

"The Goddess took our daughter," Dhenora whispered, sobbing now as she fell limp against his chest. "I couldn't forgive her."

"You didn't just insult the Goddess," he said. "You insulted Her daughters, me, and our crew." He released his hold on her and steeled himself as he turned his back and walked through his parting sailors. They fell back into place behind him, preventing her from following.

As much as he knew she wanted him to do it for her, he couldn't drop her overboard. He closed his eyes, head bowed, and waited.

No one spoke, and no one moved. His sailors gave her that much respect, at least. It was a long time until he heard the splash.

His ship abruptly lurched forward to the natural feel of the wind and current, yet Bhurati wept.

Afterward

Captain Bhurati's Last Voyage is one of many stories I started and never finished because I didn't know where it was going, at least until I was looking for 'one more story' to include in the collection.

When I started it, all I had was a basic idea to kick it off - a ship at the mercy of mermaids, but little more than that. I totally forgot about it until I stumbled across the story while digging through some old story files.

Fortunately, what I rediscovered was the beginnings of something with promise. Several drafts later I changed who was responsible for the story's main problem and it all came together.

MERRIE DAWN

A SCIENCE FICTION SHORT STORY

Terrence looked at the scrap of plaspaper again, reading the handwriting by the nearby glow of an illuminated wall. *Merrie Dawn, Centerian Complex, Corivan Road – after hours only.*

His breath frosted in the air as he studied the brightly lit building across the street, a sense of despair settling over him.

He coughed, grimaced, and then wiped a spot of silver-flecked blood from his lips.

The sign read: *Merrie Dawn's Relaxation Chamber.* "This can't be right," he muttered.

A whorehouse.

He crushed the plaspaper in his palm, shoved it into his trouser pocket and walked away in disgust.

His friend, Narrenden, must have written it down wrong. Must have. There's no way an empath would or could work in a whorehouse.

The emotions would be overwhelming. Then again, perhaps the empath didn't have a choice; some whores were rumoured to be slaves.

He pulled the note out and read it again. It wasn't in Narrenden's hand.

The Ophelian contact must have written the message and passed it through intermediaries.

And, it was all he had to go on to save his daughter's life. Biogerm infection and the treatments used to combat it were killing his baby daughter, Shaunen.

She'd already had a liver transplant, and now her kidneys and lungs were failing. He'd been told she only had days at best.

An empath, though, could reduce Shaunen's suffering – take the tension from her body and hopefully give her some strength.

In a few more weeks the next generation of anti-virals would be available for human testing, and he could get her on the program.

He pulled off his coat with its Federation sigil and hid it between two parked transports, then slowly worked his three marriage bands from his fingers and placed them in a trouser pocket.

With any luck his jacket would still be there when he returned. Tension made his legs weak as he crossed the street and stopped before the door.

He looked around to ensure no one was about, and then slipped inside.

Low, sensual light illuminated the foyer in warm reds and yellows. Secretive shadows helped hide and selectively reveal the curving architecture, alcoves and throughways.

Human and Ophelion men and women lounged in preparation for customers, ignoring him. Most were naked except for the colourful ink decorating their bodies – a popular attraction among many of the peoples of this sector.

An older Ophelion female, the hostess, approached him. She wore a long blue gown of very expensive liquid nenfit.

Terrence resisted an urge to back away. The nenfit was toxic to human touch. The dress clung to her curves and reflected light on what were supposed to be the sensual parts of her bony body.

Some humans found Ophelions attractive. Exotic.

They reminded Terrence of the whippet-like pigs he'd hunted on Aarenos IV.

"What services are you requiring?" she asked in a naturally husky voice.

"Uh," he hadn't thought this far. He couldn't just ask for an empath. He'd be lynched. "Uh, a human. Female." He hoped the empath was female.

Sixteen human women moved from various alcoves and drifted toward the centre of the room.

They'd been chosen for their beauty. He studied their faces, features perfectly balanced, all young, yet nothing alike.

Their hair varied from blonde to black, with skin in various shades of pale to ebony. He had to remind himself they were probably debt-slaves or at best received payment for their services in accommodation and food vouchers.

And he was married.

He frowned. He'd once seen a crewwoman beaten in the street

after openly asking for directions to an empath. "I'm looking for a gentle girl," he said.

She pursed her grey lips, as if smiling. "All our girls are gentle, should you wish it. Anything else?"

He fought an urge to run fingers through his prematurely greying hair. "Uh, I want a full night." He glanced at the slave girls. "Massage, conversation." His ringless fingers suddenly felt naked. "Sensuous pleasure, perhaps."

The hostess smiled, careful not to display her short tusks before a prospective human client. "Of course," she said.

She waved her arm toward the girls. Two drifted away, returning to their positions by the walls and alcoves. The others obediently formed a line, all smiling, some suggestively, some coyly.

"Anything else?"

His palms began sweating. "Not really," he said. Asking for *someone who radiates an aura of calm* wasn't going to help. "Friendly, perhaps…"

His breathing was beginning to feel constricted again, but if he coughed now, showed any sign of illness, they'd throw him out just on the suspicion he had biogerm infection. He took a deep breath and let it out softly.

"Insightful," he finished.

The hostess nodded. "Our girls are trained in all the finer arts, including relaxation therapies and substances, conversation, music, dance and specialised performances." She waved toward the remaining women. "They are all friendly and insightful. Please, choose."

Only one girl caught his full attention. She had dark hair, olive skin, and a dimpled smile he found irresistible. Much like his wife before biogerm ravaged her vitality.

As he met the girl's eyes, she looked away. Teasing. Good. He couldn't afford to choose someone he felt attracted to. He made to turn from her, but noticed the gold and silver tattoos decorating her breasts and crotch. He stared. Not ink. *Biogerm* tattoos.

She should be dead.

"Her," he blurted.

The hostess smiled. "Of course. No man can resist Merrie Dawn."

Terrence blinked. "Merrie Dawn?" His fingers brushed the pocket with the handwritten note.

Merrie Dawn looked up, her smile failing to touch her eyes as she studied his face in return. Terrence pursed his lips.

She stepped forward, welcome abruptly radiating from her posture and expression as no doubt she'd been trained to show.

He tried to return his attention to his hostess, but the gold and silver of Merrie Dawn's biogerm tattoos distracted him. He *had* to question her about them.

"A wise choice." The Ophelion hostess held out a recscan. "Please confirm our transaction with your credit slip. Full fees will be charged prior to any services being provided."

He balked at the amount, more than he earned in a week. He could lose Federation-funded medical treatment, not to mention his position, as well as face the possibility of criminal charges if he went ahead with this. For the chance to save his daughter though…

He swallowed, and with a shaking hand paid with an anonymous slip.

"Thanks," he said, and then wondered why he was doing the thanking.

The hostess smiled, forgetting to hide her tusks. "Merrie Dawn, please accompany our new guest to your chamber."

He followed Merrie Dawn up an old-fashioned flight of stairs, brushing his fingertips against the invisible shielding used to prevent customers falling from the edge.

He needed to touch something to calm his nerves. Gold and silver biogerm dragons ran up the backs of Merrie Dawn's legs, gold on the left, silver on the right.

He wondered if she'd known the risks when her masters had forced them on her. Incredible. She must have had major reconstructive neural surgery and a host of new organs along with an extensive rebuild of her nervous system.

She waited for him at the top of the stairs, then took his arm and led him along a circular corridor. He stiffened at her touch, but forced himself to relax. She couldn't still be toxic – the tattoos looked like they'd healed a while ago.

"What's your name?" Merrie Dawn asked.

She had a soft voice, youthful, though he couldn't determine her age. She was probably augmented in every way conceivable.

He couldn't resist dropping his eyes down her front. The body-work biogerm tattoos on her breasts looked like dragons, each about to bite a nipple.

At her crotch, another biogerm dragon offered oral pleasures.

He looked away, reminding himself he was married. "Terrence. My name's Terrence."

"First time?" she asked.

His heart skipped a beat. "Pardon?"

"First visit to a Relaxation Chamber on Ophelia?" she asked.

She stopped, and a door decorated in flower motifs slid open.

"Is it that obvious?" he asked.

Gods, she was beautiful with those dimples. If he wasn't married, or a Fed staffer...

"You seem nervous. Embarrassed, even. I take it you're from a world with standards that frown upon my trade?"

He cleared his throat. "Something like that."

She smiled, slipped her hands behind his neck and stood on her toes for the briefest of kisses. Peaches. His wife, Kirrin, tasted like peaches.

He stiffened and pulled back, but she'd already moved to the door. He touched his lips, wondering if the kiss had been enough to infect her with biogerm. He looked up and found her watching him carefully.

"Enter," she murmured, leading the way in. He suspected she'd been about to say something else.

As soon as she turned away, he let himself breathe again.

Of all the cursed luck...

He looked at the doorway. Just a simple step, but oh so significant. He cleared his throat to avoid a cough and touched his ring fingers, then stepped into an open and spacious room.

"Are you okay?" Merrie Dawn asked. She was watching him again. Studying him.

"Fine," he said. "Low blood pressure." The truth, at least.

"You look pale."

"Just a little dizzy. It's nearly passed."

Discreet lighting brightened the chamber as he wandered toward the centre of the room.

A large four-poster bed dominated the far side, while real, old fashioned curtains of red and gold cloth decorated the walls.

"Expensive," he whispered.

"What were you expecting?" Merrie dawn asked as he stopped before her.

"Uh, to be honest, I don't have a clue. Images? Sensory equipment? I don't know. Mirrors maybe?"

She smiled. "All possible, should you ask."

She brushed her fingers across his shoulders as she circled him, stopping close enough to kiss him again had she been on her toes.

He met her eyes. If a slave, she put on a very good act. He almost thought she wanted this more than her customers.

She took his hand in hers and gently caressed his fingers. "I take it you're after something your wife can't give you?"

With a jolt, he snatched his hand back, the shock ramping up his heart-rate. His rings had left pale impressions on his skin, and she'd noticed.

He took a deep breath and let it out slowly. He should have expected it. He swallowed hard and stepped back slightly. "Can we just talk for a little while? We've got all night, after all."

A secretive smile spread across her face, and she raised an eyebrow ever so slightly. "Of course."

She walked slowly to the bed, her naked body moving sensuously. "It's your money."

She touched a flower motif on the bedpost. Energy hummed. She leaned forward and slid into the air, floating above the bed.

Surprise replaced his annoyance. He gave a low whistle. "The service industry must be profitable for you to afford gravity displacement generators."

She smiled. "The joys of being on a trade world. Trade is booming."

She pulled several pins from her hair and let the dark mass float free.

"Despite the fact Ophelia's been implicated with the spread of biogerm?"

"Yes." She rolled over and gave him a long, penetrating look. "I thought Federation personnel were forbidden to visit Relaxation Chambers?"

He stared, his body stiffening. How...? "I assume I'm not the only one to break the rules?"

He met her eyes but she gave nothing away.

A smile finally played across her lips and flirted with her pale blue eyes. "Perhaps," she said, pausing dramatically. "Ophelia's not yet a member of the Federation. Fortunately. *We're* not legally required to turn anyone away, or to ask."

"Despite the risks?" He was thinking of biogerm, not politics.

She smiled and ran her fingers over her biogerm-decorated breasts. A momentary sense of paranoia made him wonder if she knew what he was thinking. It didn't help that he found watching her floating above the bed extremely erotic.

"The rewards are worth it if you know what to look for."

"Rewards? I don't follow."

She rolled over in the air again. "Obviously," she whispered.

He crossed his arms and looked down. "So what's your story?" he asked. "Refugee?"

When she didn't answer, he looked up. She was watching him like a predator.

He shivered.

She changed her position once more and slid to the edge of the gravity field, gently using the post to pull herself free of its influence. She approached and slowly circled him.

Terrence remained still, trying to disguise his discomfort.

Gentle fingers brushed him, caressing his back, his chest, sending pin-pricks of erotic excitement along his skin.

"Relax," she said.

He felt flushed. Breathing seemed difficult, and it wasn't from his biogerm infection.

"I need to know something," he said. "Are-"

"Am I an empath?"

He twisted from her arms and turned to face her, backing away. "How?"

Her dimples deepened as she smiled like a fox. She took a step forward, forcing him to move back again. "I allowed you to meet me. I take it the tattoos were the giveaway?"

"You're the Ophelion contact Narrenden spoke to?"

A secretive smiled showed off her dimples, but she didn't answer.

"So you're screening me for someone else then?"

She raised an eyebrow. "Do you want to save your daughter?"

He looked around the room for surveillance equipment, suddenly sure he was being set up. "I'm leaving."

"Walk out that door now and your body won't ever be found," she said.

He stopped, disbelief keeping him momentarily speechless. He met her eyes, and saw she meant it.

"If you have something to tell me, then say it."

"Why would a lab technician with federation-funded medical benefits risk everything to find an empath?"

"An empath might be able to help my daughter."

Merrie Dawn gave him a steady look. "And you'd trust one, knowing what harm their perversions can do?"

"Shaunen'll be lucky to see out another day or two without one. I have no choice."

Merrie Dawn raised her chin slightly. "There's a sampler by the door. Place your hand on it and let it confirm your identity, then give verbal permission to record this session."

He shook his head. "Not a chance. I won't leave any court-permissible evidence."

"I thought so. I've had it with you Federation spies. Get out."

His jaw dropped. What had he stumbled into? Empaths were reviled, not spied on.

"I'm sorry. I've come looking in the wrong place, obviously." He turned and headed for the door.

"If you're telling the truth about who you are, give my sympathies to your wife for the loss of your daughter."

Terrence stopped by the door, rested his head against it, and sighed. If there was any chance she could lead him to an empath, he needed whatever help she could offer.

"What do you get from this?"

Her dimples returned with the smile that flirted on her lips. "I'm taking a gamble. This has nothing to do with your daughter."

"What then? My position as an assistant biogerm researcher?"

"Let's just say that some people like things the way they are."

"You're talking about a cure, aren't you? If you have one, then tell me. If it works it could be distributed across the entire Federation within a year."

"If that were true there wouldn't be a biogerm problem, and I wouldn't have to keep my identity hidden behind the name of this business."

She had a cure! "What is it you fear? Exposure as an empath?"

She shook her head. "I'm not an empath, at least not in the traditional sense. I'm not a 'sensitive'."

"Then why the elaborate set-up?" He gestured at the room angrily.

"I need to keep my secrets close. I have to be certain of who you are. Your intentions."

Resentment clashed with fear and hope. "Tell me. Please," he whispered.

"Touch the sampler by the door or this goes no further. If you're concerned about a record I'll erase it as soon as the sampler confirms your identity. No recordings, I promise."

Another risk, but he'd come too far to back out now. He clenched his jaw and touched the sampler's node. He felt the tingle and removed his hand when it finished.

They waited several seconds before his official file appeared as a hologram in the middle of the room. An image of him turned slowly while statistics screened through the air.

The only thing missing was his positive biogerm status – something he'd so far managed to keep off his official record.

The end of his file displayed holograms of his wife and daughter and their biogerm status – type silver. The display stopped there, and after a few seconds winked out.

"Erase the last query please," Merrie Dawn said.

Done, a feminine voice responded.

Merrie Dawn looked at Terrence. "Happy?"

He frowned. "Are you?"

"I'm far from happy to be risking exposure, but I'll disappear after our meeting. Can't take the chance you'll reveal my presence."

"You want something from me. What is it?"

She raised her eyebrows. "Many things, and none."

"You think you can blackmail me? You want access to Federation research?"

"No. The biogerm treatments you help develop are the problem, not the solution."

That implied only one thing. "Sabotage?"

"No," she said softly, almost under her breath. "All I can do is help you take life to your daughter, if you think the risks are worth it."

"Then you have a cure."

"No, but it's better than anything your Federation is using."

He had the feeling she wasn't saying something.

"We're working toward a cure, and thanks in part to my team's research, a new anti-viral treatment should be in production by the end of the Federation year. They've proven to be far more effective against both biogerm strains than anything available now."

She leaned closer, whispering so softly he barely heard. "What makes you think biogerm's a virus?"

"Because..." Because that's what he'd been told. Evidence implied it. Research confirmed it. He frowned, suddenly uncertain. "It acts in ways similar to other alien viruses which affect humans."

"Yet it's not."

"But-"

"Trust me, it's not."

He began to speak, but she touched his lips with a finger.

"What would you do if I help you – save your daughter's life?"

"I have no money to speak of."

"I don't want money. I'm rich enough."

"Then what do you want? I won't betray the Federation."

"Two things. Firstly, a promise you won't tell anyone."

He raised his eyebrows. "You can't be serious? A cure for biogerm? Everyone should know."

"I have my reasons. You'll understand when you know about it, and not before." Her face was unreadable.

"Tell me!"

"Either you make the promise, or leave."

He closed his eyes, an image of his dying daughter in his mind. "I promise," he whispered. "So long as you deliver what you say you can. What else?"

"Good enough. Secondly, make love to me."

"What!" He opened his eyes with a start, shaking his head. "There's no way-"

She touched his lips again. "I'm sorry, but your promise isn't enough. I need insurance. If you break your promise I can ensure you face Federation court for contravening the moratorium on Relaxation Chambers. Though, somehow, the possibility of a note finding its way into your wife's hands would be more likely to keep you silent. That's the deal. Take it or not."

"Even if I agreed, which I won't, you should know I'm infected with biogerm. The silver strain. Infection could kill you unless your cure is real."

"I appreciate your honesty, but I knew that when I kissed you earlier." She held her palm out before him, and blew white powder into his face just as he was breathing in.

He yelled and moved back, blinking tears as he wiped it from his eyes.

"What was that?" It tasted like liquorice. He wanted to spit.

She moved to the far wall. "Something to make this easy. What world are you from?"

He paused, wondering where she was leading. A wave of dizziness hit him. He gasped and dropped to his knees. "What did you blow at me?"

"Just a mild hallucinogen and memory suppressant, combined with an aphrodisiac. It'll wear off in a few hours. So now, tell me who I am."

He couldn't think. The room was wavering no matter how many times he blinked. He tried to stand, but stumbled and hit the ground.

He closed his eyes, wondering how he got so drunk. It must have been a big night, and not just alcohol. His head throbbed. He couldn't even remember going out.

He looked up. His wife was watching him from the far curtain.

"Kirrin?" He had trouble focusing. He frowned, pushing himself to his knees. "What are you wearing?"

"Terrence, I need you to think carefully. Where are you from?"

He frowned. "Arim Noriethir. As are you. Where are we? This isn't our room."

Kirrin parted the draped cloth to reveal a small terminal.

"Arim Noriethir, clothing, female, underwear. Casual, sensual, and traditional."

Her body hid the images, but he could see the reflected light on the side of her face and shoulder.

Any audio feedback must have been going straight to her implant. Kirrin raised an eyebrow and pursed her lips as images cycled through. Goose bumps prickled his arms.

"What's going on?" he asked as he pushed himself to his feet. The dizziness was going.

She walked over to him, a hungry look on her face.

"I thought you were sick. Have you gone into remission?"

He coughed, and grimaced at the taste of blood in his mouth. He suppressed another cough out of habit, though she knew he'd been infected at the same time as her. He'd infected her, after all. His body was merely dealing with it better. He frowned. Or was. She looked healthier now than him. Much healthier.

She approached close enough to brush her breasts against him, ignoring his question. "All fairly boring except for the corsetry."

He thought briefly of the first time he'd ever made love to her. She'd been wearing a beaded corset as part of an ancient musical performance, and he'd never fully undressed her. She'd had a waist he could put his hands around, then. Before biogerm. Before Shaunen.

Kirrin's nipples brushed against his shirt. "I think it's very erotic."

He took another look at her strange clothing. Not clothing. Tattoos. When? How?

He stepped back, staring at the tattoos in sudden shock. Biogerm tattoos. They must be new.

How come she wasn't dead?

He tried to remember. The tattoos would take days to kill. The toxins must be affecting her mind.

He felt the sexual intensity radiating from her, and found himself responding despite his best efforts not to. But just touching her would allow his skin to absorb toxins from her body.

She noticed his fixation, and smiled. "They're old. No longer toxic. Forget about them."

He tried not to pull away as she put her hands behind his neck and drew his head down next to hers.

Whispering, she said, "I might have something 'traditional' in my range I could put on. Shall I?"

Please, he thought, yet found it difficult to think past her tattoos. When had she got them? "I-"

"Of course you would." She smiled. "A moment." She slipped behind the curtain.

Terrence raised his hand but she was already gone. His heart was beating hard. He took a deep breath, then another, suppressing a cough.

What was going on? He was responding like a teenage boy. He closed his eyes and massaged his temples with the heels of his hands, trying to think it through.

He walked over to the bed and sat down, but a gravity field began lifting him.

"Wha!" He grabbed the post and pulled himself free. He couldn't remember when they'd had that installed. He needed time to think. Lots of time.

"A decade ago empaths were respected."

Terrence spun around, but couldn't see Kirrin. She remained behind the curtain.

What was she talking about now?

"I still respect them. One helped my grandmother. What of it?"

"Ever stop to consider why there's been such a turnaround? Why would empaths, who are often so sensitive they're unable to harm even someone hurting them, suddenly be linked to every crime imaginable?"

Terrence shrugged. "I haven't given it any thought."

"Because certain people want it that way. Very powerful people. Those with a lot to lose. Turn around."

"Why?"

"Because I asked you to."

He sighed, wondering if she'd deliberately misinterpreted his question. "Fine." He turned. "Those aren't really tattoos, are they? They're just imitations."

He heard her step through the curtain and approach him. He began to turn, but she spoke first.

"Don't, please." He listened to her come closer, and before he could react her arms snaked around his waist and pulled him tight to her.

"Relax," she said. "And don't worry about your biogerm infection. It can't hurt me."

What was she talking about? She had it too. The warmth of her body penetrated his shirt. Her arms relaxed slightly and her fingers began to trace the lines of his chest.

"You're acting strange today," he said.

"Shhh. If you don't like it, say so."

He closed his eyes, took hold of her wrists and pulled them down and away. He knew what she'd be wearing and felt himself responding accordingly, but he had too many questions.

He released her arms with the intention of stepping away, but her small hands slipped around his wrists and guided his hands back to her body.

Somehow, he couldn't resist her gentle strength.

"Please, not yet," he whispered. Perspiration trickled down his forehead. "Something's wrong."

"Then stop me," she said.

Just one touch. No more. His hands found her sides and his breath caught. Soft silky fabric cinched her waist. He moaned.

"You like it?" she asked.

Despite himself he nodded. He turned within her arms... and caught sight of her.

She again pulled his hands to her waist. The gold garment pushed Kirrin's breasts up, exposing only half of her gold and silver dragons.

He ran his hands up her stomach, and found he couldn't resist touching her decorated flesh. Her skin felt soft, the dragons almost hot under his fingertips.

She breathed in sharply. "The tattoos rarely warm to the touch," she whispered. "If only you were looking for a life partner again."

"Huh?"

She touched his face, her hand feverishly warm. There was a new look in her eyes. Passion.

"What a surprise you are." Her hands slid up behind his neck, then he felt her fingers through his hair.

"When did you go into remission?" he whispered.

She paid no attention; pulled him down into another kiss. Peaches.

Her scent invaded his mind. His eyes rolled back and he closed them, unwilling to pull away.

She broke the kiss and her lips moved to his neck.

"Is this a dream?" he wondered, not sure if he spoke the words aloud.

"Not a dream," she whispered. "More like a wish."

He ignored his instincts and picked her up.

She kissed him as he carried her to the bed and they allowed the gravity field above it to draw them in.

She unbuttoned his shirt agonisingly slowly, playfully fending off his attempts to kiss her again.

Unable to think of anything but the heat of the moment, he fumbled at his pants until she helped him remove them.

As his clothes floated away, she wrapped her legs around him and they feverishly joined, her skin exotically hot.

He breathed in with shock from the heat of her body, then kissed her again.

They rolled in the air, moving in rhythm as perspiration quickly coated them.

Her fingers dug into his back, scratching all the way to his buttocks.

He moaned, moving faster, all thoughts turned toward her.

An abrupt thrill passed through him and her legs tightened behind his back, forcing them hard together.

His breath caught as he released.

Seconds passed, a moment so intense he couldn't think, couldn't breathe.

As it passed they stayed entangled, floating above the bed for minutes as the moment slowly dwindled away.

He could barely keep his eyes open, barely think. Stray drops of perspiration floated in the air around them.

She smiled. "In all the time I've been doing this, you're only the third partner I've reacted to like this."

That didn't make sense, but he couldn't work out why.

He felt thirsty, hot. Incredibly dizzy. He closed his eyes, ignoring her comment. He felt exhausted.

He imagined her smiling as she ran her fingernails down his side, then slowly, teasingly disengaged.

Her free hand caught his cheek as he opened his eyes.

A smile slowly spread across her face.

"Time to wake up," she said.

She reached out and touched a small sensor above the bed. Sweet cool air cycled from vents by the posts.

"I never said I had a cure."

He frowned. "What?"

"The name's Merrie Dawn, remember? At least, it is tonight."

He shook his head, not understanding. "Kirrin, are you...?"

Kirrin's form resolved into that of Merrie Dawn, and his clouded memory became clear.

"Shit!"

He pushed away, but the gravity field only extended to the edge of the bed.

"What did you do!" he floated back.

"Relax." She smiled. "You wanted to save your daughter, didn't you?"

A thrill of fear passed through him. "Yes. No. What are you talking about? What did you do to me?"

A burning sensation began in his groin, then a sharp pain drove through his stomach. "Argh! What did you do?"

She laughed, actually laughed. "Best I don't say. Trust me."

He felt her amusement, but the words didn't make sense. The pain slowly subsided, leaving him light-headed.

"I feel... strange."

"Drunk?"

He tried to push her away, but couldn't untangle her arms. "Let go," he slurred. "What did you do?"

"Shhh. Don't fight it."

He looked around the room, trying to focus on the curtains. On anything. What had she said?

"Fight what?" he couldn't breathe. Couldn't think. "I'm dying," he whispered.

"No. Relax and let it explore. Join with it as you did with me."

Join with it? "I thought you were Kirrin," he slurred.

"Only while you needed her."

"Kirrin?" he whispered.

He felt pressure against his mind, a presence trying to soothe him.

He rolled in the air, his eyes momentarily focusing on the silk sheet above him. Below him.

Someone's hand stroked his forehead.

He looked around, found himself floating, the room slowly rotating around him. "Where am I?" he whispered.

"Shhh. You're safe. Relax."

He began to feel a warm, gentle presence beside him.

"Kirrin?" his eyes closed of their own accord. "Kirrin, it's been so long. Hours. I should have come home sooner."

"If you like." A soft hand cupped his cheek. "Relax now."

He laughed and let her comfort him. "They told me you were infected with biogerm. The silver strain. Like Shaunen. Like me. I knew it wasn't true."

A finger traced the lines on his forehead. "Shush dear. Go to sleep. I'm here for you."

He relaxed, letting unconsciousness take him.

Slowly, like waking from a long cryo-sleep, he became aware of his wife beside him. The gravity field was off and they were lying on their bed.

A smile slowly worked across her lips. She stretched languidly, naked, her biogerm dragons moving sensuously.

"Welcome to my world," she said. "You've been asleep all night. It's nearly dawn outside."

He marvelled at her dimpled smile, her perfect body.

But then he frowned. She looked different. Younger. Healthy. When did she get the tattoos?

"Open your eyes," she said.

What? Shock forced an intake of breath. He opened his eyes and sat up. She lay beside him, just as he'd imagined. Only it wasn't his wife. Merrie Dawn. Guilt wrapped itself around his heart and squeezed.

"You didn't imagine it," she said. "You can see with your mind now."

He gaped. She was reading his thoughts.

"Only your surface thoughts. You'll work it out. I told you I was telepathic, sort of."

He felt a strong sense of the room, and most of the building and people nearby. "What have you done to me?"

"You don't need to thank me."

No, he didn't. He felt it in his soul.

"The biogerm?" He touched his groin. "Gold strain?"

She smiled. "Of course."

"They work together? I can feel you, sense your presence." He touched his head, feeling the presence of thousands more like himself, if not where they were. "There are others on this world."

"Many. If the Federation knew how many, we'd be exterminated. The biogerm changes us when the two strains come together."

The scientist in him had to know, guilt over his wife or not. Out of energy already, he lay back beside her, palms massaging his eyes. "Tell me."

"There's little to tell. Biogerm's basically an alien fungus. It produces male and female spores – gold and silver." Her fingers brushed her biogerm-derived tattoos. "Gold passes on through sexual contact, silver via saliva. They spread, find a 'mate', and mature into a new organism. That begins a new symbiotic relationship with the host."

"But the spores sicken and kill people!"

"Yes, but only when infected with a single strain. The spores replicate like a virus, which causes problems – cellular damage, autoimmune diseases, organ failure."

A good reason to find a cure, he thought. He couldn't keep the sarcasm from his voice. "And this benefits the host, how?"

She smiled in a patronising way, which made him want to grate his teeth.

"Symbiosis gives the host the ability to communicate telepathically with other hosts, to sense emotions, to see with the mind alone. What's more, our bodies no longer see the biogerm as foreign. Had your wife achieved symbiosis before giving birth, your daughter would have been born with a natural immunity to it which would have lasted until she reached sexual maturity."

The implications began to come together. "But surely the authorities must have known this…"

"The ones that matter, yes."

"Yet they keep it a secret! Why?"

"Who makes money from treating biogerm? Who's got the finances to control the spread and stop it becoming common knowledge?"

Almost a whisper, he said, "Federation companies producing antivirals and other treatments."

"The sickness industry. It's called 'making money'."

Merrie Dawn rolled off the bed and walked to the curtain. Reaching through, she grabbed something and returned. She held out two small vials containing a greenish-gold liquid.

He knew what they were. "Live biogerm shots," he said.

They were used to inject animals for scientific research.

"So you understand then. To save your daughter, you risk her persecution. Saving your daughter will put both your life, and hers, at risk. Now you know why I wanted insurance. They may be monitoring you. When you leave here, you'd best hide your new knowledge, and symbiosis."

He took the vials, staring at them as if at poison. "Kirrin can make her own decision, but Shaunen…" He looked up. "How can I?"

Merrie Dawn leaned forward and briefly kissed him on the lips. "I don't know. Just keep your promise. You can tell your wife, but only so long as she promises to keep the secret, and you don't tell her about me. Leave by the front entrance. You'll find your Federation jacket there. I sent someone out to pick it up."

He left the room, his new awareness spreading out before him. Once downstairs he could sense the street outside. Narrenden was there. It took only a moment to understand why.

Terrence had been used. They were after Merrie Dawn. Some friend.

He searched the building with his mind, but Merrie Dawn, or whoever she really was, had left already. His biogerm senses found several other exits and two passageways underground. She could have left by any of them. To do the same, however, would risk exposing his own knowledge.

His mind caught several people entering through the rear entrance. They kept out of general sight and spread out, two heading for Merrie Dawn's chamber, two more to the building's comsystem.

He smiled. Merrie Dawn wouldn't have left any records of their encounter on file. He doubted she'd have even taken any with her, either.

He picked up his jacket and left by the front entrance, as expected. He crossed the street, head down, pretending he didn't see Narrenden.

It took only a few metres before his 'friend' caught up.

"Terrence! Wait!"

Terrence turned, pretending surprise. "What are you doing here?"

"Thought you could use a lift. My transport's just here."

They stopped before an official Federation vehicle. The windows were one-way, but he could *see* two people in the rear seats. He made sure his eyes never looked directly at either as they stopped before the door.

He smiled. "A lift would be great. Thanks."

He reached into his pocket and pulled out the biogerm shots.

"Hey, look at this. I found the empath – she grilled me all night and even had me pull my file. Talk about nervous, though I can't say I blame her. Still, she refused to come to the hospital, but she did give me these. She claimed they're a cure."

Narrenden took them. "Med-shots? Best get them analysed. Could be anything in them." He pocketed them. "I'll let you know by midday. Don't count on anything though."

He slapped Terrence on the back. "Hop in. Got a couple of friends in the rear – needed a lift to the lab. I'll introduce you on the way. We swung by on the chance we might cross paths. They're good guys. They promised not to say anything about the whorehouse."

Terrence had no trouble faking relief. "I appreciate that."

On the flight to the lab Narrenden joked about the possible sexual exploitations Terrence may have had during the night, attempting to draw out a confession.

Terrence laughed at the last one. "Well buddy, that would make it ten last night. Even you're not that good. Or are you?"

Narrenden chuckled. "Maybe."

Terrence closed his eyes, feigning tiredness. He relaxed his senses, felt for an impression of Narrenden's mind as opposed to the two men in the back, then sifted through the man's surface thoughts. Strangely enough, Narrenden really did regard Terrence as a friend.

The image of a pinhead camera on Terrence's jacket abruptly crossed Narrenden's mind. The bastard! Some friend. Luckily Terrence had left the jacket outside the Relaxation Chamber.

They landed outside the lab. "Well," Narrenden said, "Looks like we'll have to keep searching for an empath to help your daughter." He gripped Terrence's shoulder, squeezing. "Don't worry, she's a strong girl. With any luck, she'll go into remission. I've seen it before. And those new antivirals will be out soon."

Terrence nodded, looking Narrenden in the eye. He tried to express the infinite hope only a parent could hold.

"Thanks. I'm sure she'll be fine. You know, I swear there was more colour in her face last night. Maybe the last dose of treatment is finally kicking in."

Narrenden nodded dismissively. "I've got some business to take care of, but I'll see you in the lab this afternoon." He paused, showing concern. "Hey, why don't you take some some time off and visit your wife and daughter this morning? You look tired."

The transport floated away.

In the office, Terrence did a few hours' work, and then took Narrenden's advice and headed to the hospital. As he walked through the front entrance he slipped a hand into his jacket pocket for reassurance. A new jacket.

His pockets were filled with medshots of both gold and silver biogerm, filched from the stores kept for animal experimentation.

A lot of people were going to go into 'remission' today to hide his daughter's unexpected recovery.

It was the only way he could think of to draw attention away from her.

That was today's problem.

Tomorrow he had to work out how to contaminate medical supplies with biogerm.

Perhaps in the next few months he would apply for a transfer. He'd heard Production had some openings.

Research, after all, no longer held his interest.

Afterward

The idea for Merrie Dawn came, oddly enough, after a visit to the Polynesian Cultural Centre in Hawaii (because that's an obvious connection, right?). While I'm certainly no expert on Polynesian culture, the concept of tattoos being a respectful part of family and cultural tradition resonated with me. That 'respect' aspect became entwined with empaths, which left the tattoos as secondary, but still important.

The other part of this story stems from my views on what I perceive to be a rapidly growing culture of business and political leaders putting self-interest ahead of the people and society they're supposed to serve and lead.

When self-interest gets out of hand, nations tend to fall. You don't have to look too far into the past to see examples of this, or find signs of the same things happening now. GFC, anyone?

The problem these days is, while today's nations will rise and fall as all nations do, many have nuclear weapons. There will be consequences.

FLASH FICTION

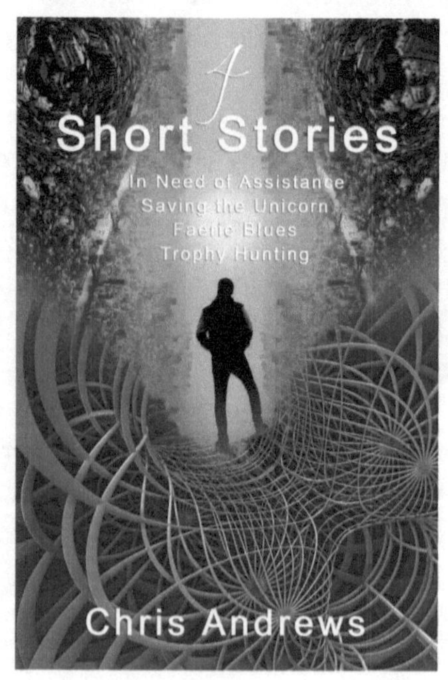

"So what do we do now?" Brin asked, staring at the smartly-dressed faerie they'd locked in Lennie's rusty old bird cage.

The honey they'd used to lure the faerie into the trap was all over the creature, sticking its wings down.

"Shake it," Lennie said excitedly, reaching for the cage. "Faerie dust doesn't just come off by itself."

Brin pulled the cage aside. "It's all sticky. We need to clean it up first."

The faerie crossed his arms and glared at the pair until Brin got the hose and sprayed him.

High-pitched squeals answered the drubbing. Afterward, the faerie picked itself up, still glaring, but now both sodden and sticky. It shook itself, one wing eventually coming unstuck, and then the other.

"We're going to have to wait for it to dry out now," Lennie said, completely unimpressed. "And it's still a bit sticky. Maybe you should hose it again?"

The faerie began looking worried.

"And risk washing all the faerie-dust away?"

"It'll make more. Go on, hose it. It's your fault there was too much honey in there anyway."

"Maybe we could give it a bath?"

The faerie looked really worried now. He reached into a pocket and pulled out a phone. After giving it a shake to make sure it wasn't water-logged, he dialled a number.

Brin and Lennie stared at each other in surprise.

"Hey, Tink?" the faerie said. "Peter about? There's a couple of snotty-nosed brats that need some time aboard Captain Hook's ship. Great! See you soon."

Lennie swallowed.

"Maybe we should let him go now," Brin said, opening the cage door.

Afterward

This little bit of fun flash fiction came from my childhood when plastic bug catchers were a thing. You'd spend half your day chasing butterflies and grasshoppers, only to let them go and do it all again.

This story reminds me of those long summer holidays.

ANY JOB IN A HAZE

A VEIL OF GODS SHORT STORY

Sara flicked the cigarette butt under the hopper opposite her. Despite a slight shake in her hands it went where she'd aimed. Crouching, she rested the back of her head against the wire fence, trying to ignore the beginnings of withdrawal and the service bay's reek. She'd slept in worse.

The hospital's rear door opened. Her brother, Ben, walked out with a couple of bags of trash, his white hospital uniform clean and his hair slicked back. Vain as always, the ass. He stopped and glared when he saw her. "What do you want?"

She stood, trying on her best smile, the one she used when begging office workers for change in the city. "I need work, Benji. I'm trying to clean myself up." It wasn't entirely a lie.

Ben glanced at her street swag and ratty clothes. "You missed Emma's birthday. Again."

Bastard. She knew he'd hold it against her, but the guilt hurt anyway. "I was detailing cars that day."

He gave her a *bullshit* look before dumping the trash in the hopper. "Emma's five, Sara. She needs a mother, not a junkie."

"What big brother gives drugs to his thirteen-year-old sister? What chance did I have?"

"I cleaned up."

"While you kept supplying me and took every dollar I could beg or steal." She dug inside her jacket and pulled out a present, gift-wrapped and everything. She threw it to him.

"What's this?" Ben asked as he caught the pink-wrapped box.

"A necklace. Real silver. I even got it engraved with Emma's name." She'd been carrying it since Emma's last birthday.

"Stolen?"

"Screw you. I paid for it."

He threw it back to her. "Give it to her yourself then."

"I didn't steal it Benji." She kicked her street swag with her boot. "I'm living alone and I need money to get off the street. I want work. I'm hungry, Benji. I haven't eaten in two days. I'm clean and I want to stay clean." She really did want to straighten herself out. It was just so *hard*.

His features didn't soften. "What'd you do this time? You only get like… Did you overdose again?"

She hunched against the wire fence. Time for another sob story. "I was in the city a few weeks back. Mum and Emma walked by."

"Mum snubbed you? I'm not surprised."

"She didn't even recognise me. It's my twenty-first birthday next week Benji…" she trailed off, wishing she knew what she wanted to say. If she wasn't off the streets by her twenty-first she wasn't ever likely to be. A few years ago she'd told herself it was her eighteenth.

"Emma asked Mum to bake a cake for you. She's already told everyone you're coming home because it's your birthday. She said the same thing on her own birthday and cried herself to sleep that night. I've got a long list of disappointments if you want to hear them."

"Keep your list, jerk." Sara pushed off the fence and picked up her street swag – her only possession besides the clothes she wore. She wasn't going to listen to another rehash of her crimes. She should have done this in the foyer so she'd have the satisfaction of embarrassing him.

"You really want work?" he asked.

She gave him a flat stare. Considering the number of times she'd let him down she shouldn't be surprised. "That's all Benji."

He held her eyes for a long moment and she wasn't sure she liked his expression. "I'll see what I can do." He had that calculating look which told her she was about to get screwed again. If she'd had anything to her name she might have been worried.

"Thanks bro. I owe you one."

"You owe me dozens. If you can't make a go of it this time don't come back."

She owed him alright. A kick in the guts if he was ever down. "You've said that before." She began walking.

"Piss off, Sara."

She gave him the finger over her shoulder.

"Where are you going to be?" he called.

"Belco. I'm going to try the car yards."

Hours later, Sara had made her way through half the businesses trading in the top of the town centre, but couldn't even convince a hairdresser to let her sweep the floor for enough change to buy a coffee. The way she was going she would have to screw some old married bastard for her next hit.

Catching her reflection in a shopfront window she doubted she'd be able to attract a zombie. She needed to get to a shelter and clean herself up. Contemplating a short step off a busy overpass as a better option, she didn't see the limousine pull up until the door opened in front of her.

"Oy! Watch it jackass!"

"Perhaps if you were a little more polite you'd have a job by now," said a woman with an English accent.

Curious despite herself, Sara glanced in. "Who said I was looking for a job?" A well-dressed dark-haired woman studied her in return. She couldn't have been much more than Sara's own age, only with long legs and a killer body to match. Business suit. Heels. Diamond necklace. She could have been of Italian descent despite the English accent. Sara would have killed for the woman's breasts – one flash and they'd have purchased her anything she wanted.

"Your brother."

"How do you know my brother?"

"Get in or keep walking. I'm busy."

Sara gave the woman another long look. Maybe she could sponge something off her. "Better than a career as a road pizza," she muttered, getting in and dumping her street swag on the leather seat beside her. If her brother was involved it was probably semi-legit. Sanctimonious, ass-kissing prat. What the hell did he know about working in a hospital anyway? Probably screwed his boss to get the job.

She glanced around the interior. Plush carpet. Polished wood. Fairy lights in the roof. Flash. Expensive. Smelled new. She stiffened at the sight of a dead body slouched at the far end of the limousine, but the woman only gave Sara an amused look. What was Benji into?

"I have a job opening."

"Dead boy there's a job opening?" The gloom of the interior hid the details of how he might have died, but his suit seemed perfect. Expensive. No knife holes or obvious bloodstains.

"Close the door, Sara."

"That's a dead body. I should call the cops." Hopefully the woman would pay her a few bucks to say nothing.

"I suspect the police know you better than they know me, so leave if you like. I won't stop you." There was a fancy metal bucket of soft drinks in ice next to her and little packets of nuts and pretzels. Her stomach told her to stay though it was more than food she craved.

"How'd he die?"

"I drained his lifeforce. Succubi do that."

"So he slit his own wrists out of boredom?"

The woman gave a slight smile. "Shut the door so we can discuss my proposal, Sara. No obligations."

Sara glanced at the food again. "Can I have something to eat?"

"Help yourself."

Sara shut the door and grabbed a packet of nuts as the limo left the curb, stuffing them in her mouth in case the woman changed her mind. She opened a can and took a huge swig. After a minute the woman shifted position, swapping one dark-stockinged leg over the other. "I thought you'd walk, to be honest. Consider your first test a pass."

"Who are you?" Sara asked around a mouthful of nuts. "How do you know my brother?"

"Your brother works at the local hospital, and hospitals are a wonderful source of... well, they're a place where a lot of people pass away for all kinds of legitimate reasons. I sometimes help them move on. A while back I introduced myself to your brother and now we assist each other. He's very good at distracting the right people at the right time. So far he's proven himself trustworthy, a quality I appreciate."

Trustworthy? Bullshit. "Sure. I guess." Sara glanced at the body again as she finished the nuts. She reached for a packet of pretzels, but hesitated with her hand halfway out.

The woman smiled. "They'll only go stale, so take as many as you like."

Sara opened the pack, tempted to stuff a few more in her pockets. "What do you want from me?" Why did she feel like she was sitting in a cage with a lion?

"I'd like you to help my driver carry Sebastian into the catacombs when we arrive. The local ghouls are getting hungry and there's plenty of distilled lifeforce remaining in Sebastian's flesh. They're very good at cleaning up… problems. Otherwise, how do you feel about being a donor?"

Catacombs? What frigging catacombs? "Donor? You wouldn't want my blood."

The woman smiled. "I need your *lifeforce* dear, not bodily fluids. Consider it whoring – after a fashion."

"I don't whore." Unless the money was really good and she needed a hit.

"There's the lifeforce of course, but I promise you'll enjoy that. Also courier duties, making appointments, taking calls, cleaning up the occasional… mess, and anything else a personal assistant would do. I'll expect discretion, of course."

"Personal assistants give… lifeforce stuff? And clean up-" she snuck another glance at Sebastian. "Mess?"

"Mine do."

"What he do?" She'd seen a couple of dead bodies and he didn't look much different. Less wasted.

"Sebastian lacked loyalty."

"So you killed him?" Sara could be wrong, but with her eyes getting used to the gloomy interior she thought Sebastian might have some bruising around his mouth. There was a little blood on his collar too. No, not blood. Lipstick. The same dark red the woman wore. Was it too late to back out? "What's in it for me?"

"Food. Clothes. Immortality perhaps."

Sara gave her a *screw you* glance.

"How about free bed and board? The first six months will be on a trial basis, but after that you can expect a very nice salary and a killer wardrobe. You'll be on call twenty-four seven, mostly nightshift, but you'll be rewarded for that too."

"Sounds perfect for someone who just escaped an asylum. I'm more a *hire-for-parties* kind of girl."

"Then perhaps you're not the assistant I'm after. Shall I ask the driver to pull over?"

"I'm just trying to avoid another night in a cell, that's all. And whoring. I'm very particular about whoring. I prefer men anyway, not... suca... girls."

The woman sighed. "How about private school for your daughter?"

"You'd send Emma to private school?" she asked, experiencing a weird sense of hope.

"Full fees, uniforms, excursions, everything. I'll even throw in a sweetener; if you stay for at least five years Emma's schooling will continue until she graduates. All on me. You'll need to be discreet *and* loyal, of course. I'm not trying to trap you Sara, or coerce you. I'm a honey-pot kind of succubus, but I do demand loyalty."

"And Sebastian wanted a bigger honey pot?"

"He wanted the hive."

"Private school," Sara whispered, and money for drugs – and anything else she wanted. No more living like a beggar. "What's your name?"

"Tammy."

She'd expected something more snobby, like Diana, Princess of Limousines. "Okay *Tammy*. I'm interested."

"Good. I'm in the market for someone who doesn't ask questions, does as they're told, and acts within my best interests. I'm also looking for someone who won't be missed should things go sour like they did with Sebastian here." She reached out to shake on the deal.

Sara sat a little straighter. "That sounds threatening."

Tammy smiled. "Only the truth. I'll expect nothing less in return should you work for me."

"The truth? I've seen that movie and it didn't end well for the army guy."

"Perhaps Sebastian should have watched it?" She glanced at her hand, an eyebrow raised and waiting.

What did she have to lose? Her life was shite anyway. Sara shook before grabbing another packet of nuts and finishing her soft drink. It was a while before the limousine slowed and pulled over, gravel crunching under the tyres.

"Second test. Help my driver carry Sebastian inside."

Sara bit the inside of her cheek, battling second thoughts as footsteps approached her door. She suspected this was a succeed or die kind of a job, but it might be her only lifeline to her next hit. After that she could disappear if she had to. "Yeah, okay. I can do that."

As Sara opened the door to bright sunlight someone slugged her across the jaw.

* * *

Sara awoke on a bed with a thumping headache and a handcuff locking her right wrist to a tubular steel bed-head. Her jaw ached. She tugged at the cuff, fear blooming.

"Finally."

She knew the voice. "Benji?"

"Hey Sara." Ben moved to her bedside, staring down at her like he always had. "I thought Tammy would drain you the moment you told her to shove it. You did tell her to shove it, didn't you?"

Sara pulled at the cuff again, the metal rattling in the stark room. Concrete walls, no window, one door. "Where are we?" The place smelled of disinfectant, like a hospital. She'd woken up in enough emergency rooms to know.

"Tammy's always talking things up. She slips me a little money every now and again and expects me to be happy with it. Someone else slipped me some money recently, a shitload of it, and all I had to do was drop her location this afternoon..." He rubbed his thumb against his fingers. "I honestly thought Tammy would have taken one look at your pathetic ass and dropped your carcass into the catacombs with Sebastian. Two stiffs for the price of one."

"Tammy's going to kill you."

"When they finish interrogating her, *she's* going to die. I got bumped up the loyalty list. By tonight I'll be so rich I can do whatever the hell I want. You've gotta know who your friends are, sis."

"Why am I cuffed?"

He picked up a full syringe from the table behind him. "Payback for all the shit and embarrassment you put me through. I want you suffering from withdrawal symptoms so bad you'll beg for death, with the cure only a few feet away. I'm sick of you dogging my ass all the time, begging for handouts."

"Look in the friggin' mirror if you want to see the cause of my situation."

He put the syringe back on the table, well out of her reach. Shite, she already had muscle aches. It wouldn't be long before she was in full withdrawal. She needed that syringe.

"I'll inject you after you get through the worst of it to start the process all over again. Sweet dreams." Ben winked and left, locking the door to the room.

"Asshole!" she yelled. Sara pulled at the cuff once more, but the metal merely rattled. "Crap." She got up, determined to drag the bed over to the table and get the syringe, but its legs were bolted to the concrete floor. Bastard. She got back on the bed and kicked the bed head. "Ahh!" She kicked again and again, losing her temper and growing more and more desperate for that syringe.

Metal cracked and her hopes surged. The weld had fractured.

She kicked again and it split. With a little effort she got the cuff free and rushed to the table, picking up the syringe as she pulled her sleeve back.

Tracks lined her arm, but she didn't care. She slapped her elbow to bring up a vein before plunging the needle through her skin.

She almost pumped it in, too, almost, but she couldn't help herself if she was messed up. If she could keep her head clear for a couple of hours she might get out of this. All she had to do was get through the door. "Friggin' easy," she muttered.

She withdrew the needle and threw the syringe at the wall. To ensure she couldn't change her mind she stomped on the thing, and regretted it instantly. Shite, she should have kept it safe for later. She shoved her hair out of her eyes, the loose handcuff rattling across her face.

So nobody could use it to cuff her to anything else, she put the other half over the same wrist and locked it into place. It wasn't like she'd never been cuffed before. She'd had a boyfriend who liked that sort of thing. She could pick it later.

She found a small storeroom beside the door. It held a mop and bucket, a broom, cleaning equipment, a plunger, and a crowbar.

"There is a friggin' God," she muttered as she grabbed the crowbar and used it to jimmy the door open. Splintering wood cracked loudly as the frame around the lock gave way.

When nobody came to investigate she slipped out and made her way along a dimly lit service-corridor under the building. The last door before the stairwell was ajar. She carefully glanced in and gasped in surprise. Tammy lay on a wooden bench against the far wall, her wrists cuffed above her head and her ankles cuffed to the opposite end. There was a needle in her arm too, draining her blood into a bag sitting on dry ice. Three bags were full already and Tammy was deathly pale.

"Mother of weirdness," Sara whispered.

"Sara? Help me. Please," Tammy said weakly.

Sweating as much with nerves as withdrawal symptoms, Sara cautiously walked over.

"The keys are on the bench," Tammy whispered.

Sara pulled the needle from Tammy's arm before unlocking the cuffs and then her own. How the woman was still alive she didn't know.

"Pass one..." Tammy pointed to the blood bags as Sara helped her sit. "Please."

Hesitantly, Sara grabbed a bag of blood and handed it to Tammy, wondering how she was going to inject it back into her veins. Tammy's fingernails grew sharp and she punched one through the bag. The blood turned black and thick before drying to powder inside the bag.

"Eww!"

"The rest. I need my strength back. All of it."

Fighting the urge to cringe, Sara handed the remaining blood bags to Tammy who did the fingernail thing again. Colour returned to the woman's face, although not as much as before.

"Oh, that's just wrong," Sara whispered, fascinated despite herself.

Tammy smiled, and Sara finally noticed the woman's teeth had grown dangerously sharp. Sara fought an instinct to back away. "More." There was a smear of blood at the corner of Tammy's mouth. She must have bit her own lip in some sort of rapture.

"That's all there is."

"I need more lifeforce. I'm weak without it." She focused on Sara with disturbing interest.

Sara backed a step. "You can play vampy-thing all you like, but I'm leaving."

"Sara, there's a dozen supernatural creatures upstairs, some of them far more deadly than me at the moment. They'll kill you before you make it to the street. We need each other. I only need a little of your lifeforce. I promise I won't harm you."

Sara eyed the woman's lips, red now, rather than drawn and pale.

"You really are a succubus?"

"Yes."

Sara heard the footsteps a moment before her brother walked in. "Sara?"

Sara backed away as two huge men strode in behind Ben, both easily twice Sara's weight. Tammy yelled and ran at them, but the men caught Tammy's wrists and slammed her against the ground with the sickening crack of bone on concrete. Tammy didn't move after that.

Sara almost fell out of the way as they picked Tammy up and dumped her back onto the table, cuffing her hands and ankles again. One of the men put the needle back into Tammy's vein while the other pocketed the keys and grabbed Sara.

"Please," Sara whispered. The man's fingers bruised her skinny arms as he pinned them behind her.

"Silly, sis," Ben began as he grabbed an oxygen mask attached to a small canister from the table. "This should take the fight out of you until we can find you another room."

Sara struggled. "Benji, please. I'm trying to straighten out!"

He caught a handful of her hair and used it to control her as he forced the mask over her mouth and nose. She tried to hold her breath but the other man punched her in the stomach. She doubled over, taking a breath of something sickly sweet. Her head started spinning as her knees collapsed and she nearly passed out right there.

Ben removed the mask.

Sara tried to speak but the man threw her to the concrete floor. She hit hard and rolled, slamming into the wall. She wanted to puke.

"I'll be back when we sort out another room," Ben said. Locks bolted into place. Trying to focus, Sara got to her feet and staggered over to Tammy.

"Hey! Wake up." She slapped Tammy's cheeks to rouse her. The woman's skin was cool. Too cool.

Tammy's eyes opened slowly and it took her a long moment to focus. "Are you okay, Sara?" Tammy asked.

"Yeah," Sara lied, surprised the succubus even considered her welfare. Her teeth were normal again at least. Despite her spinning head Sara managed to remove the needle from Tammy's arm, but without the key or a thin bit of metal from a hairclip she couldn't do anything about the cuffs. Maybe it was the head-spins, but Sara felt an insane urge to kiss the woman.

"Lifeforce," Tammy whispered. "I need..."

Sara grabbed the slowly-filling blood bag and put it in Tammy's hand. Tammy punctured it with a sharp nail and the blood turned black and powdery in seconds.

"More. I need to heal. I can break the cuffs, but only if I'm strong. Really strong. I need more lifeforce."

Sara leant on the wooden bench, trying to think clearly. "Benji made me breathe something..." At least it was taking the edge off her withdrawal. Maybe if she gave Tammy some of her blood they might get out of here. Staggering, she found an empty jar on the bench but accidently knocked it to the ground where it shattered. "Crap."

"Sara, I'll need everything you've got."

"Everything?" Sara swallowed in a dry throat as she turned back to Tammy. "Well, that was a crap choice getting in your car then, huh?"

"Help me and I'll help your daughter."

She made it back to Tammy's bench, leaning heavily on it. "Benji's going to kill me Tammy."

"Think about your daughter, Emma. Help me and I swear I'll keep her safe. She'll have everything you could ever want for her."

Emma was all she had left. Strange how she regretted not being there for her now. She had screwed up in the worst way possible. "Will you really get Emma into private school?"

Tammy nodded.

Sara grimaced, trying to convince herself. "Yeah. Okay. At least I can do one thing right before I die."

"You'll need to lay on the bench beside me so your body doesn't pull away when you pass out." She tugged at the cuffs to illustrate.

"You're making this very unappealing, you know that?" Regardless, Sara fought down a new wave of dizziness as she struggled onto the bench beside Tammy. This close, the succubus smelled good, really good. Tammy was a total turn-on and she had to resist kissing her right there.

"What do I do now? Put my wrist against your fingernails?"

"I can drain your lifeforce that way, but it's inefficient and better for paralysing people. You'll need to kiss me. Last words?"

"You're all friggin' heart." When Tammy didn't respond, Sara tried to think of something to justify her pathetic life. "Tell Emma I know I screwed up, but I wish things were different."

"What mother wouldn't care? Kiss me Sara. I promise you'll enjoy it."

Feeling entirely awkward, Sara hesitantly pressed her lips against Tammy's cool ones. They tasted sweet, like over-ripe fruit. A thrill rushed through her like the first time she'd screwed a boy behind the bike shed at school, and suddenly she couldn't kiss deeply enough. She ran her fingers through Tammy's hair as numbness spread through her own body, a deadly, aching kind of numbness, but she wanted it more with each moment. She kissed harder. She needed it.

"Look after Emma," Sara whispered as she took a breath. "Tell her... Tell her I love her. I really do."

She kissed Tammy once more, her lips more appealing than any addiction she'd ever known. As she ran out of breath she collapsed across the succubus.

* * *

Sara opened her eyes.

The room was too bright but her head was clear. She squinted. Down-lights. She was in someone's bedroom. Someone with a lot of money. Velvet curtains, thick carpet, art on the walls, antique furniture.

"Happy birthday, Sara. You've been unconscious for nearly a week. I was beginning to think you weren't strong enough to pull through. I almost completely drained you."

"Tammy?" Her voice was croakier than usual.

Tammy wore a long red dress, split along her left leg. The top half of the dress revealed enough cleavage to stop a man's heart at a hundred paces. "The job's yours if you want it."

"Job?" She had trouble remembering anything.

Walking like sex on steroids, Tammy turned towards the door at the sound of a commotion. Sara wanted another kiss more than any hit of heroine she'd tried.

Someone pushed Ben through the door, his wrists bound behind his back and his skin grey and tight. He glanced at Tammy, then Sara. "Oh shit," he whispered. He tried a smile. "Tammy. It was a joke. Right? What you did to me can be reversed, can't it? You know I'd never betray you."

He'd become gaunt like someone who hadn't eaten in a week.

Tammy focused on Sara again. "Your brother betrayed me."

"I remember." All Sara wanted to do was kiss Tammy and sate her growing sexual desires. "Why am I so horny?" Why was Tammy turning her on?

Tammy smiled. "You could have left me to die, denied me your help or turned back to drugs. Instead you gave me your life. Draining you cleared you of your addiction, but it means you traded one drug for another."

Sara stared. "You mean I'm addicted to you now?"

"I always reward loyalty, Sara. Emma's schooling has been taken care of and your brother's fate is yours to play with. I had him turned into a ghoul so you can do almost anything to him and he'll survive."

Sara stared at Ben. He looked dead. That'd piss him off pretty good already. Still, she was *hungry*, but it was a need only Tammy could sate now. Tammy held out a small gift-wrapped box. Emma's necklace.

"Your daughter needs you Sara."

Sara watched Tammy, wanting her. Needing her. "You couldn't control Sebastian and want to be sure this time. I'm an addict so you made sure it's you I'm addicted to you."

"No Sara – that need will pass in a couple of months. Like I said when we first met, you're welcome to leave, but the job's yours if you choose to stay. Honey-pot girl, remember? There'll be no kissing until you no longer need it, understand?"

"Private school for Emma," Sara whispered to herself. "And revenge on Benji." She smirked. "Shit yeah, but no bullshit about not kissing you, okay?"

Tammy smiled as if she'd just won something. "Deal."

Afterward

While many of my short stories are written to explore ideas and world-building concepts, Any Job in a Haze is different. It's primarily a character study loosely based around the people I'd often see hitting people up for 'food' or 'bus' money. When you see the same people week after week, and knowing Australia has a very good (okay, that's subjective) unemployment benefits scheme which financially supports the unemployed, you can be reasonably sure they're not after 'food' or 'bus' money.

All I knew at the beginning of the story was that Sara was a drug addict, her personal demons were her biggest problem, and she was struggling to deal with the consequences and get herself out of the situation.

I did want some sort of a happy ending for her though, considering how hard her life's turned out, but I didn't want to give her an easy way out either. No free passes - she's earned most of her problems and has to earn her way out.

For Sara, it's easier to get wasted and forget her problems or pretend she doesn't care than face them and the shame of her situation, so I gave her a situation where she had to step up or go under.

While I had no idea where the story was going when I put Sara in that service bay to speak with her brother, I wanted her situation to feel real and for readers to care about her, despite the fact she's not a particularly likeable character at face value.

For that to happen, she needed to make a stand of some sort and be rewarded for it, even if it didn't make everything perfect.

Consequently, Sara's a character I'd like to revisit in the future to see where she's at. Your guess is as good as mine. Hopefully she'll be doing all right.

URBAN MAGIC: APPRENTICE

A VEIL OF GODS SHORT STORY

"Tony will see you now," the young female assistant said with an interested smile.

Mick felt his pulse beat faster and smiled back, but he wasn't here to date girls. He wiped his palms on his jeans and stood, hesitating just a moment before he entered the office.

Tony's big meaty hand engulfed Mick's as they shook, then Tony pointed to a chair as he closed the door.

"How can I help you Mick?" he said as he took his own seat. "What kind of insurance are you after?"

Mick glanced at the hard-plastic chair before dropping onto it. He crossed his arms and pushed further back into the back rest, wishing for padding and feeling a need for something solid around him. Something protective.

He wanted to wipe away the perspiration on his chin and upper lip, and he wondered if he should have had a shave today. He found it hard meeting Tony's direct look. "Um, I'm not after insurance, sir."

Tony raised an eyebrow which had more hair than the top of his head. "I'm an insurance agent, Mick. If you don't want insurance, why are you here?"

The question contained no trace of irritation or annoyance to Mick's ear, yet he flinched as if rebuked. "Um." He scratched his head. "I saw you. Last night?"

Tony's expression seemed to change without a muscle moving. "You'll need to be a little more precise. Leaving work? Having a drink with a friend afterward?"

"I saw you pick up that cat in the alley. It was hurt real bad. I saw it get hit by the car."

Tony lent back in his chair. "And you saw me put it back down before it ran away?"

Mick nodded. "I know what you are. I got a friend-"

Tony raised his hand and shook his head just enough to stop him. "What is it you want Mick?"

Again, there seemed to be no trace of malice, just a simple question, yet there was an underlying threat Mick felt deep in his bones.

He hunched further into his chair. "I want to be a mage or wizard or whatever you call yourself. Like you."

Tony frowned. "I don't need an apprentice Mick."

Mick rubbed his palms on his thighs again. "I want to learn, sir. I ain't gonna say nothing if you say no. I won't tell no one, I promise, but a friend said I'm gifted and I should find someone to teach me."

Tony remained silent for a while, then folded his fingers together and leaned forward. "Can you see auras, lad?"

Mick nodded. "Only strong ones, like when people are angry. Sometimes I know when terrible things are going to happen beforehand, like when my cousin rolled his car." He looked down. "Bad things, usually."

Tony sighed, leaning back in his chair again. "I'll consider teaching you if you're prepared to do whatever I ask, no questions. First though, I need you to pick up something for me. Think you can do that?"

Mick looked up with a hint of hope. "Sure. Anything!" He pushed himself to the edge of the chair. "What is it?"

"A woman, Wendy Sivers, owns a white teardrop crystal on a silver chain. Go see her and bring me the crystal. I'll need it this afternoon." He wrote down an address and handed it to Mick. "She lives in a serviced apartment two blocks from here. There's a reception desk in the foyer, but you don't need to stop. It's not a secure building."

Mick stood and accepted the address. "Why do you want the crystal?"

Tony gave him a hard stare before speaking. "I believe I said *no questions.*"

Mick dropped his eyes. "Sorry, sir."

Tony sighed as if it wasn't important. "The crystal contains a measure of magic. Without at least one measure you cannot learn what I have to teach you. Your gift alone is not enough. You cannot see the world for what it is as you are, not really, and it will be a long while before you can. The crystal is the first step toward that."

"Oh." Mick pocketed the scrap of paper with the address. He knew where the apartment building was. "I'll be back right away."

Tony held up his hand, forestalling him. "I have several meetings between now and then. You can come back this afternoon after three pm."

Mick left and walked the two blocks to Wendy's residence. He had no trouble with reception and took the lift to her floor. It wasn't until the elevator opened and he stepped out that he realised he didn't know what to say. Hopefully she was expecting him.

He knocked and waited a moment before a young woman opened the door. She was dressed in a black mini-skirt, skimpy green top, and enough make-up to cover the face at Luna Park. She wore the silver necklace and crystal.

"You're Wendy?" he blurted, thinking she didn't fit the occult image very well. Her blue-green eye makeup was way overdone, and the mango lipstick shone with gloss. He wondered what she looked like under all the warpaint.

She smiled, but there was an edge to it. "And you are?"

Mick hesitated. "Ah… Tony Ellis sent me. For your necklace."

Her lips pursed and the smile left her eyes. "Really? Which orifice did he want it embedded in?" Mick's jaw dropped, but she cut him off. "On second thought, tell Tony he can have it with my compliments - after I've discharged its measure about a year from now." She smiled again, though this time there wasn't any warmth in it. "He'll know what I mean."

As she began to close the door Mick quickly said, "I know what that means. The crystal's not for Tony, it's for me. He's going to teach me and I need to be able to see magic... stuff, or something."

She raised her eyebrows. "You want *my* measure of magic?" She laughed. "Perhaps I'll let you earn it," she mused. "A decade of service should be enough. Depending on how you go I might give it to you then. You can start by polishing my car with your tongue." Her smile didn't come across as inviting, not even a little. "I've got plenty of dirty dishes you can get started on after that, so hopefully your tongue's not too sore. I need some shopping done too. I'll write you a list. You can pay. Perhaps tonight you can help me with a few occult works I've got in progress. Nothing too hard. I could siphon the energy you'll provide though. Good experience for you." The wicked smile deepened. "Perhaps I should have found a helper decades ago."

Mick stepped back. "I'm sorry, I-"

Wendy laughed again. "I thought so. Get lost kid. I don't take in strays." She slammed the door in his face.

Kid! She wasn't any older than he was. At least, she didn't look it. Angry, he stormed off down the hall and left the building, intending to give Tony a few choice words for humiliating him. He stopped about half way back and swore under his breath. Tony was in meetings until later.

Mick sat on a concrete post in an alley way which was put there to stop traffic entering a walkway. He clasped his face in his hands. What now? He wasn't prepared to steal from the woman to get her necklace, particularly not if she had some power herself.

He didn't know anything about magic, but he wasn't going to risk a curse or death for the chance to learn from an asshole that'd probably use him more than teach him. For that matter, it probably wasn't sensible to tell a real sorcerer what you thought of him either.

He stood and began walking, thinking through his options. It had been more than three years since he'd become aware he was gifted, and as far as he knew he'd never seen another mage or magic user or whatever they called themselves. This could be his only chance to learn. He had to get that necklace.

His only options were to buy it or steal it. He didn't have any money anyway, and for that matter she wasn't likely to sell it.

That meant thief, something which made him feel sick.

He heard a loud impact and a headlight breaking, and turned to see a woman crash to the ground on the far side of the road. A car sped off.

He memorised the number plate before running across the road at the end of the alley. He knelt by the woman and checked her neck for a pulse. She groaned as he touched her.

He breathed with relief, not realising he'd been holding his breath. Another car pulled over and a couple of men in business suits got out to help.

"Call an ambulance!" Mick called to the first man, who pulled out his mobile phone and dialled. Mick turned back to the woman and swore in surprise. It was Wendy. The necklace clip had broken and the crystal rested on the ground half hidden by her hair.

Feeling like the thief he was about to become, he quickly palmed the necklace before the second man arrived and began checking for her pulse.

"She's alive," Mick said. "But I think she might have broken bones."

Mick was quickly ushered to the side as his partner made the emergency call. Within a minute a dozen people were getting in the way in their attempts to help. Mick took the opportunity to disappear. Nobody noticed.

Down the street he bought a soft drink and sat on a bench in the shade to drink it, feeling sick and excited at the same time. His meeting with Tony was a good half-hour away yet, but he grinned. He'd done it! He didn't have to do anything bad, like break into her apartment. Finders keepers.

He pulled the crystal out of his pocket hoping to catch a glimpse of its magic, but it looked like any other cheap and tacky crystal he might find at a market, except for the silver chain. Although gifted, he could sense no aura or anything else that might imply its power.

He slipped it back into his pocket and finished the drink, then began making his way toward Tony's office. He wondered how Wendy was. He didn't particularly like her much, but he felt some responsibility for her because he'd found her.

He considered going back but she'd be gone by now. Ambulances weren't that slow. He did have the number plate of the car that hit her though, but to volunteer that information he may get discovered with her stolen crystal necklace.

He stopped walking, feeling guilty again. "I didn't steal it. She lost it," he muttered angrily, touching the crystal. He'd never taken anything dishonestly before and didn't like the way it made him feel. He felt dirty. Knowing the number plate of the car that hit her wasn't making him feel any better either. He would need to tell the police.

His shoulders slumped in defeat and he turned around. He was going to be late to see Tony, but he had to give the info to Wendy at the hospital. The police would probably be there too. The staff at least. Wendy would probably be unconscious for a while and the police gone by the time he could get there.

What if she was awake though, and wanted to know where her crystal was? She'd know it was him, for sure. At the very least if he turned up as a witness she'd be able to find out his details, and then she'd definitely know. He could lie, but he'd always been terrible at his. No poker face at all.

He ran his hand through his hair, wondering what to do. Perhaps he could drop a note with the number plate in her letterbox, or slip it under her door. He made his way back to her apartment and stopped at reception.

"Do you have letterboxes?" he asked the old man behind the desk.

"No, but I can take messages and parcels. This is a serviced apartment block. Some units are rented out, so the person you're after may have left already. I can forward a message if that helps."

"I have a message for Wendy Sivers then. Can I please borrow a pen and paper plus an envelope? It's confidential."

The man looked him over before handing him the requested stationery.

"Thanks," Mick said. He quickly wrote a brief note and slipped it into the envelope, sealing it and handing it to the man at reception before leaving. He hadn't signed the note or left any contact details, but he wasn't concerned. The crystal weighed on his conscience though. He should have put it in with the letter.

He clenched his fist, thinking about the magic he could learn with it, but he felt too guilty.

He returned to the apartment block. "Can I have that note back please? I need to add something."

After the man handed it over Mick tore a small hole at the top corner and pushed the necklace inside until the entire chain disappeared, and then handed it back to the man.

Mick's jaw dropped when he saw Tony where the man at reception had been.

"Congrats kid. You passed the test. Come upstairs and meet my sister, Wendy. She's much nicer than she might have let on."

Afterward

When I was digging through my short stories to find the right ones to put this anthology together, I'd almost completely forgotten about the Urban Magic stories hidden in a subfolder on my computer.

I'm glad I rediscovered them, as a lot of the Veil of Gods story universe, at least the parts set on Earth, came out of these concepts. While I didn't develop them into any longer works or explore the darker side of the world, they did let me explore the potential of magic in a world where there is little, and what little there is isn't flashy.

The idea for Urban Magic: Apprentice followed a television show that will remain nameless, but it was something I thought had the potential to say some important things about people and society, but didn't.

Short Stories
In Need of Assistance
Saving the Unicorn
Faerie Blues
Trophy Hunting
Chris Andrews

"I can smell his liver cirrhosis from here. Why can't I eat him? I'll be doing the world a favour."

"The human world maybe, but it won't make any difference to us."

"Right now I'm hungry enough to suck the blood from a three-day old corpse. What about her then? She smells healthy. She's beautiful. Sexy. She's got it all."

"Absolutely not."

"Why? Because she's young and pretty?"

"Partly."

"That makes no sense! I can't take a dying alcoholic and I can't have someone young and healthy. Why?"

"Just keep looking."

"I've been looking for an hour. You keep saying no."

"Because you're looking at the wrong things. Try thinking like a trophy hunter."

"Trophy hunter? Seriously? Why don't you pick someone for me and explain the reasons when I'm sated?"

"Him then, but you don't get to eat until you can tell me why I chose him."

"That's unfair!"

"You want my protection or not?"

"Fine. Because he's overweight?"

"Nothing to do with it."

"He's in his mid-twenties. Is that it? His age?"

"Partly."

"I don't know then! Because he has coffee breath? Because he's wearing a wedding ring? Because his blood smells like last week's vegetable soup? Because his hair's receding? Because he's a serial killer who secretly likes knitting with intestines? I don't know! What?"

"You got one of them right."

"I did? Which one?"

"Figure it out or you don't eat. I've already given you a hint."

"What was the hint?"

"Trophy hunting."

"He's hardly a trophy. Average looks, average build, average height. Maybe smarter than he appears, maybe not. What am I looking for?"

"I used to hunt elephants for their tusks. The bigger the tusks, the better. There are a lot of elephants being born these days without tusks, and that's a problem for trophy hunters."

"Even if I cared about elephants and tusks and trophies, he's not any of those things! All that stands out about him is that his blood smells like watered-down piss. He'd be my last pick."

"Exactly! Do you want a world filled with humans like him?"

"Eww! Of course not."

"Then you've got to clean the gene pool occasionally. Get to work."

Afterward

In case you had a big night and you're a little dusty, this is a conversation between two vampires discussing dinner options.

It was published in AntipodeanSF quite a while ago.

While the point of the story is obvious, what you may not have noticed is that it's entirely written in dialogue.

A VEIL OF GODS SHORT STORY

"Who the Hell are you?" Jack rasped, staring. His left arm moved weakly as he tried to point, upsetting the various tubes and monitors keeping him alive.

Sanandrial sat on the edge of the hospital bed. "A volunteer. A friend perhaps. Sanandrial's my name."

Jack turned away. "Piss off, old fool. I've got no friends." The oxygen coming through the tube under his nose wasn't enough for his diseased lungs, and he struggled to breathe for a few moments.

Sanandrial smiled compassionately, hoping the old man would see a little more of his own worth. Jack had been a community leader once. Respected. Honoured. What remained of him had become bitter and angry at the world since his wife had died. "Of course you do."

Jack spoke through gritted teeth. "Then where the Hell are they?"

Sanandrial raised an eyebrow. "You left them, remember?"

Jack closed his eyes for a moment, trying to breathe normally. "Go away old man, and take your morals with you."

Sanandrial lent forward, his palm hovering an inch above Jack's chest. "Cancer has infested your body. It squeezes your heart and invades your organs." He could sense it, a darkness born of self-loathing, hate, and years of physical abuse.

Jack narrowed his eyes. "What the shite are you saying? I had a heart attack, and the chest infection isn't helping."

"Yes. You did. Coughed up any blood lately? Been vomiting? Chest pain?" He ignored Jack's stunned look and stood to take an unopened flower from the bunch on the shelf. "Flowers. I thought you had no friends."

"Work sent them."

"Ah." Sanandrial sat on the bed again and rested the bud and stem across his left palm. He smiled. "This bud wants to flower before it dies, but it won't without help. It was picked too young." He concentrated, sent a little life-force through his palms, and the bud opened into a yellow rose, small and perfect. "Fortunately help arrived."

"Nice trick." Jack said turning away. "I've seen better. Can you wave your hand and make it disappear, too? Make yourself disappear while you're at it."

Sanandrial ignored the sarcasm. "Only with it's Permission." He hoped the hint would be enough. "How old are you Jack? Fifty?"

"How do you know my name?"

"It's on the medical information sheet at the end of your bed." Sanandrial said, smiling.

Jack glared, clearly wanting to be left alone.

"What the hell do you want?"

A smile played across Sanandrial's lips. "Wrong question." He glanced out the window. "You know, I visit a lot of people here. I like to talk to the patients, cheer them up, help them out on occasion. Always makes me feel happy." He pursed his lips. "My apologies for the bad news, and I don't mean the heart attack or infection. I suggest you complain about a few more thing. Get some more tests done." He glanced at Jack's torso. "Perhaps the doctors can do something about... it." He passed the rose to Jack, who took it reluctantly. "I'll stop by tomorrow."

Jack stared at the rose and watched in shock as it opened in his hand. "What are you?"

"Someone who cares."

The following day Sanandrial found Jack in another part of the hospital. He handed the sick man another yellow rose. "How'd the tests go?"

"How did you know?" Jack asked. "About the cancer, I mean. They ran some tests and found it, just like you... hinted." He sounded like an entirely different man now. More contrite. More lost. Closer to giving up.

Sanandrial sat on the bed, sighing. For some people, that kind of news ignited something in them. Perhaps it was too early to tell with Jack. It was fresh news, after all. "Magic."

Jack stared blankly, but Sanandrial didn't elaborate.

"You some sort of faith healer?" Jack finally asked.

"No."

"Then what?"

"What would you do with your life if I could help you Jack? Keep drinking yourself to death. Keep pushing the people who care away? Die a grumpy old bastard instead of a grumpy middle-aged bastard?" He tried to put as much sarcasm into his voice as he could without being rude.

Jack stared for a long while, sunken eyes full of questions. And fear. "For the longest time I've just wanted it to be over."

"Then I guess I don't know what to do." Sanandrial stood to leave, but Jack, surprisingly quick for such a sick man, caught his hand.

"I'd apologise to my friends for being such as ass. I doubt most would forgive me. I said some horrible things. Did some horrible things. But it would be a start."

He released Sanandrial's hand. "Live, I guess. Be better. Give up the grog. I've spent so long trying to kill myself in a slow, roundabout way, but I didn't realise how badly I want to live. I always wanted to see France and Germany. Wander around their little villages. Meet the locals. See the sights. I guess I'd start with that and see where it took me."

Sanandrial smiled. "Oh, I already know where it'll take you, if you have the courage." He pointed to the yellow rose, raising an eyebrow.

Jack stared at the rose for a moment, then at Sanandrial, understanding slowly coming into his eyes. "Please," he said, granting Permission. "Please help me."

Afterward

Another almost-lost story which would have never have been seen by a reader's eyes if not for this anthology.

Like the other Urban Magic short stories here, The Touch was mostly a world-building exercise, exploring the concept of Permissions. If you've read Divine Prey, you might notice Kimbriel asking a Permission.

This was the first time I put that concept to words.

SAVING THE UNICORN

FLASH FICTION

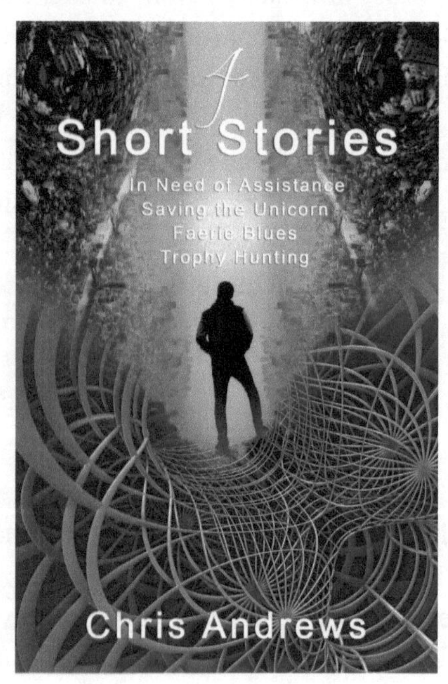

" $\mathbf{A}$ re you ready?" Master Thearris asked. "We cannot try this twice."

"I am," Augustine said.

"Good luck."

Augustine nodded thanks. "I will succeed." He activated his staff and the world shimmered. Light blazed painfully; when it cleared Augustine stood before a cave mouth — four-thousand years in the past. He gripped his staff and moved into the magic-hewn granite labyrinth, searching memory for the turns leading to the unicorn's cell.

If Augustine failed, a handful of people would control almost all magic for the remainder of this world's existence. What power he possessed now had been scraped together over thirty years. The power in his staff had taken generations to accumulate.

To Augustine fell the task of freeing the last unicorn.

He walked stealthily, cloaked under a stone illusion, blending with the walls. He hoped he had energy enough to see him to the unicorn's prison.

Perspiring with the effort of silence, Augustine slipped past several guardians holding hefty bronze-tipped spears. He moved close enough to one man to smell his halitosis.

Outside the unicorn's cell lay her mate's carcass, horn removed, body decomposing. Augustine turned away and swore a heated oath of vengeance, walking around the carcass to the wooden door.

His illusion gave out. Fully visible now, he slid the bar from the door and pulled it open quietly.

The unicorn cowered in the corner, its back whipped and bleeding. Her broken horn would grow back in time, but if she remained here it would be removed again and again to control the magic it passed into the world.

The unicorn trembled, backing further into the corner. Augustine moved in, forcing her out with his presence. She stopped when she saw her mate's body. As he followed her into the antechamber, a voice boomed: "What are you doing?"

Despite a lifetime of study, Augustine barely understood the question. He looked up.

A huge spade-bearded warrior approached, spear lowered. Augustine spoke a cantrip, heart hammering. His staff tingled with activated power.

The warrior closed. Augustine swung his staff, but the man dodged. The momentum carried his staff into the unicorn's ribs. A cascade of sparks showered the room, blistering Augustine's hands. He dropped the staff.

The unicorn screamed and fell, dead, her fur blackened where the staff struck. Augustine stared, horrified. His staff's glow faded. The world blazed.

Augustine staggered as his master's office re-formed around him — all hint of arcane knowledge and apparatus gone from the shelves and bench. In their place, unusual devices hummed, and coloured lights blinked.

"Are you listening?" Thearris asked. The master's robes were gone, replaced by a drab short coat. Augustine's own robes had changed to similar garb.

"What?"

"I said, we lost the O'Brien contract. The notice just arrived on the fax."

Augustine put his hands over his face. "Oh no," he said.

Afterward

Saving the Unicorn was written in response to a weekly challenge the Canberra Speculative Fiction Guild used to run (informally).

It was my first attempt at flash fiction, and was subsequently published in Antipodean SF.

THE PRESIDENT'S ASSASSIN

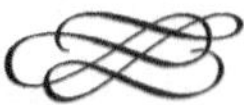

A SCIENCE FICTION SHORT STORY

"We should never have come here," Lydia hissed under her breath. "It's too dangerous."

Sarah slipped her hand in his. "I know how important this is," his daughter said with a smile. "I trust your judgement." She gave him a kiss on his cheek and with a cheeky wink toward her mother she slipped ahead down the corridor, her security detail following.

Benjamin watched before glancing sidelong at his own security team, men and women he'd trusted with his life since he'd become President a year ago now.

He sighed. "I've been very open about this. Ophelia's the only trade hub that doesn't consider our expansion a threat, and we need them in the Federation. I can't insult them by walking out now." He squeezed her hand, determined not to let the upcoming media event get away from him.

She leaned closer. "But there's an assassin out there," she whispered.

He tried not to react as they moved down the corridor, though shock coursed through him. How had she found out? "Rumours," he tried to assure her. More than rumours, but he wasn't going to confide that. His security team assured him any public event was going to be a problem.

She narrowed her eyes as if she recognised the lie just as clearly as he did. "I heard different."

He look a long, slow, calming breath. His position had enough problems without adding conflict with his wife. Without expanding trade routes to support the ever-growing needs of the colonies, the Federation was likely to implode, and there was already enough unrest thanks to the biogerm pandemic. He wanted to shield her from it all and keep her and their daughter safe and as separate from his political problems as possible. Unfortunately, it wasn't nearly as easy as he'd have liked. "Who told you?"

She glanced sidelong at Nepherian, his senior media advisor.

"Nepherian?" Benjamin asked loud enough for the woman to hear him, but she wouldn't meet his eyes. She'd probably told Lydia just to piss her off. They got along like trees and fire.

"Ben, someone wants you dead. Record the speech and do away with the pomp."

Ben lowered his voice so his security personnel wouldn't hear them arguing. "Ophelia's admittance to the Federation requires more than a recorded announcement. This world's far too important to risk offending. If you're worried, stay here."

She met his eyes and he found real fear there. "I'm not worried for me," she whispered back. She squeezed his hand almost painfully. There was little he could do to allay her fears, and despite being the most powerful man in the Federation he was powerless to put her concerns to rest.

"They're ready for us," Nepherian said as they arrived at the elevator, a finger on her earpiece.

Lydia glared at the other woman before returning her attention to Ben. "Are you using a resonance field, at least?" she asked with a raised eyebrow.

"Keep your voice down," he murmured, glancing at his security detail. He didn't want them to feel insulted. They did a brilliant job keeping him safe, and he didn't need his wife causing trouble with them.

Nepherian kept her attention on Benjamin, pretending not to have heard. "Sir, we need to head down to the lobby. People are waiting."

Lydia gripped his hand again. "Ben-"

"Not now, Lydia." Benjamin put his arm around his wife and directed her toward the door. "The announcement is being held in a secure media room. It would be easier to take out the entire building than infiltrate Federation security."

"It's been done before."

How did she know that? "Not in a decade."

She stopped walking, refusing to let him guide her out the door. "What about Sarah? What if someone tries to go through her to get to you? She's our only daughter. She could be used. This world isn't safe for any of us. Where did she go anyway?"

"Sarah's with the Ambassador's son. She has four security personnel within twenty metres of her at all times, and a full complement of guards as backup, not to mention the security from the Ambassador's attaché."

Lydia didn't seem any happier. "The ambassador's son? If she gets pregnant again I'm not paying to store another embryo. I swear that girl is going to bring your administration down all by herself."

He sighed. "She's young and in the media spotlight more than either of us would wish. Let her have her fun while she can. Come on. We have to go."

"She already gets away with too much as it is," Lydia said, but she let him guide her out the door.

They entered the lift with Nepherian and four security staff, dropping the two hundred stories in five seconds with the dampeners whining the whole way. More security personnel led them through corridors cleared of the public, the luminous walls turned up to full brightness for security purposes.

The sounds of talking reached them from the media room.

"I still think you should consider a resonance shield," Lydia said with another dark look at Nepherian, as if his media advisor were somehow responsible for his security.

Nepherian didn't take the bait, instead attaching a thumbnail-sized vocal projector to his lapel.

"Lydia-"

"I know. You're the President. I almost wish you'd never ran."

"You were the one pushing me," he countered, a little surprised by the statement. If it hadn't been for Lydia he'd have been happy as a simple planetary Governor.

"That was before I knew what was important to me. You and Sarah."

He could shield Sarah from the media circus to some degree, but Lydia took her duties too seriously, supporting him in everything. Sometimes, like today, to a fault. Despite her concerns for his safety, there wasn't like to be any real risk. Every media person and their equipment had been scanned, along with every official, the building's security personnel and staff, and anything else that might cause a problem.

"Eyes," Nepherian said as she put on skin-tight gloves and opened a small box. She touched the clear concue with the tip of a finger and held it up.

He hated the feel of the things, but held still as she pushed his eyelids wide and inserted the devices, one in each eye. He should just get implants. It would be easier. He blinked a few times to get them settled, the first line of his speech already projecting across his vision.

The concue's words bent around Lydia's worried face. She seemed even more worried than usual. The news about the threat had really gotten to her, it seemed. His security people had only confirmed the threat yesterday following the arrests of three local biogerm-infected radicals.

"This is about biogerm, isn't it?" she asked quietly.

He frowned at Nepherian again, but she gave him a mystified look and a tiny shrug. She'd held that back, at least.

"Of course not."

"Oh, come on!" Lydia almost hissed. "We're on Ophelia and the disease infects nearly a tenth of the human population. How could a death threat not be connected? People only care about trade when it fails. It has to be biogerm. Enough infected citizens believe the Federation is covering up a cure, and plenty of them want to strike out at something. You're giving them a target!"

"There is no cure, Lydia," Nepherian said patronisingly as she adjusted Ben's jacket. Lydia stiffened in response.

"Enough," he said before they could get into it. He didn't need this before an announcement. One blunder and someone would take it as an insult, and that could lead to the wrong people being offended. The Federation was already far too volatile. It wouldn't take much to see worlds rebelling or seceding.

The hotel manager caught his eye, an Ophelian with short tusks mostly hidden behind his lips. He had slightly faded gold and silver biogerm clan tattoos at his temples – old ones no longer toxic to humans. Biogerm ink was brewed from an extract based on biogerm-infected blood and distilled in a process the Ophelians refused to share. The natives appeared to have a natural tolerance to both strains of the disease and the toxins biogerm produced, something being looked into for a possible treatment or vaccination, but it still infected humans and other races at an alarming rate. The death toll was increasing.

The Ophelian nodded. Everything was prepared.

"Good luck," Nepherian said.

Lydia sighed. "Good luck honey." Despite the words, she still had *that look*, and he wasn't sure she was wrong to be concerned.

As he walked out onto the stage the assembled media crowd began yelling questions, maybe a quarter of the people in attendance human. Many raised their recorders, trying to catch his attention.

He lifted both hands, palms outward as his concue began scrolling. "I'm sure you all have questions, but please give me a few minutes first," he read.

Tusked Ophelians dominated the numbers, but plenty of other species were represented too, at least three of them vulnerable to biogerm. Despite himself, he couldn't help a twinge of nerves. Security would have scanned everyone and every piece of equipment and ensured no one infected had been given entrance, but people solved problems and Presidential security was just one.

"I'm sure you all know Ophelia has qualified for Federation membership." His concue stopped as the throng began shouting questions. "Please. You can ask your questions when I'm done."

The words began scrolling again. "As you're aware, Ophelia applied for Federation membership a decade ago today. I'm pleased to announce the Council of Federated Worlds has formally accepted Ophelia's application. This week, Ophelia's parliament will vote to ratify that acceptance and become the thirty-ninth world of the Federation."

The shouting began again and he had to hold his hands up, waiting for it to settle. He couldn't afford to let this get away from him, particularly not with the issue of biogerm constantly threatening. Silence was his most powerful ally.

"This decision will of course mean some changes here on Ophelia, but also across the Federation. We have a twenty-year transition period in which Ophelia's tariffs, taxes, trade laws and even some customs will change. As always when we welcome a new world into the Federation we intend to make the transition as easy as possible, with support at every level. There will be challenges of course, but our goal is to bring Ophelia into the Federation with minimal disruption to its people, businesses and government. You may ask questions now."

Hundreds of people began shouting, and he dreaded many of the questions. He tried to avoid the topic on everyone's lips - the spread of biogerm infection.

He chose a tall, bony Ophelian to the left, her short tusks protruding slightly and gold and silver biogerm tattoos decorating her arms. "Mr President, there's a rumour about an assassination plot. Can you elaborate?"

Trying to hide his surprise, Ben glanced at Nepherian who stood just off the stage, hoping for some sort of direction from her. The woman shook her head, clearly embarrassed by the leak. Benjamin took the hint and resorted to a well-practiced smile. She didn't want him to touch the issue. "Just rumours. Next question?" He pointed to another Ophelian closer to the front.

"What do you say to people who blame the spread of biogerm infection on Federation inaction?"

Without allowing his casual smile to slip, he nevertheless cursed inwardly. He had a feeling it was going to be impossible to dodge the issue, but at least he'd come prepared. "The Federation is doing every-thing possible to halt the spread and find a cure. Biogerm is a disease, not a conspiracy. You're welcome to contact any medical facility for further information." Hopefully that would signal his views on the subject and the questions would shift back to Federation membership.

He pointed to a human a few rows back, the man's recorder set up on a tripod. "Biogerm toxicity seems to harm humans more than any other species. Why is that?"

Benjamin tried not to grind his teeth. This line of questioning wasn't going away. "I'm not a biologist, but if you leave your card with my security people, I'm sure we can find some answers for you."

The media representative raised his hand again, not waiting. "Mr President, what I mean is that biogerm originated on Ophelia – among Ophelians. Surely withholding the cure is an Ophelian ploy to force Federation membership."

He tried to keep the surprise out of his voice. That wasn't one he'd heard before. "I can assure you there was no coercion. Ophelia is a welcome addition to the Federation. Biogerm is an inter-species disease with no cure at present. That's a confirmed fact. Please stick to the topic of Ophelia's acceptance into the Federation."

Something hit Benjamin's chest as he heard an explosive *crack*. He froze in shock before someone tackled him to the ground, their body-weight pinning him down. He felt no pain, but wasn't sure that was a good thing as panic took hold of him and everyone else in the room.

"Stay down!" the bodyguard yelled as Ben began to struggle, crushed under the big man's weight. More security personnel surrounded them before hauling him from the stage, his heart pounding in shock and growing fear. If they'd gotten to him, what about his wife and daughter? Were they safe?

It took a moment for the adrenalin to flush the shock away and be able to speak clearly. "What happened?" Benjamin yelled as they took him to a secure room where medical personnel began stripping his clothes away. "What did I get hit with?" He still didn't feel any pain, but that wasn't an indicator. Whatever hit him could have included a nerve agent. "Are Lynda and Sarah safe?"

Nepharin nodded. "They're fine."

The security guard touched his earpiece. "The assassin's dead," he said. "Shot when he tried to run."

Somewhere outside he heard Lydia abusing security person-nel, trying to get to him. He wanted to tell them to let her in, but they were just following procedure.

He was more concerned that another assassin might target her. "Who's with Lydia?"

"Tails and Grimmer."

"Make sure she's all right and let her know I'm unharmed, and then send someone to check on Sarah. In person."

"Yes sir."

A forensic medic of Karakian origin began sniffing the jacket Benjamin had been wearing while a human checked him for injury.

"I think I have it," the Karakian said, her wet nose twitching like a rat's. She pulled the voice projector off Benjamin's lapel with the tips of her sharp claws.

Benjamin stared in shock. The voice projector? "Nepherian?" She'd attached the button-sized device.

The Karakian medic shook her head. "This device probably saved your life." She used tweezers to pull a millimetre-long dart from it, dropping both the dart and the projector into separate bags. She sealed them before handing them to an assistant. "I want both analysed."

"A dart?" Benjamin asked.

"Probably fired with compressed air. It's almost impossible to detect when assembled from legitimate equipment and pressurised inside the room."

A doctor checked his pulse and breathing while another unwrapped a syringe and took a sample of his blood.

"The threat was real?" Benjamin whispered as the shock finally got to him. Worse, they'd almost got to him. He should have listened to Lydia and used a resonance field.

He spent the rest of the day undergoing tests and being questioned by his security detail. Ophelian officials came to express their horror at what had happened, while Nepherian tried to talk him into leaving Ophelia immediately.

"I'm the President. What image would that project to Ophelia and the Federation?"

It was well past nightfall by the time he arrived back at his suite where Lydia almost flattened him with a hug, and he honestly felt glad for it. Some of the tension began to melt away.

"Oh, oh, oh!" she said, sobs escaping her before she stood back and slapped his chest with both hands. "You should have used a resonance field!"

Her eyes were red, and he doubted it was the first time she'd cried today. He caught her in his arms, closing his eyes as he half buried his face in her bleached hair, breathing in the warm, familiar smell of her. "I'm fine," he whispered.

She pushed back after a moment. "Security told me you'd been poisoned!"

He took her hands, finally noticing they weren't alone. "The dart missed. I'm fine." Nepherian and two other senior advisors waited on heavily-padded leather lounge chairs, while four security people stood around the walls. More waited outside the room.

Benjamin cleared his throat. "Would you mind giving us some privacy? Please?"

Nepherian and the other advisors stood and moved toward the door with the guards, but Lydia caught Nepherian's shoulder as she passed. "Would you stay a minute please? I have a question." Her tone was cold and precise.

Ben didn't like the tone, and judging by Nepherian's expression, he wasn't likely to appreciate where this might go.

"Lydia, Nepherian's not responsible."

Nepherian glanced from Ben to Lydia as if asking a silent question. When he nodded, she smiled in an unnaturally strained way, as if the tension she normally shrugged off had found a place between her shoulder blades. "Of course."

"Are these rooms monitored?" Lydia asked when the last security guard left, her demeanour changing in a blink. It made Ben wary. Were the crying and tears a ruse for his security personnel and his advisors until she had a chance to take her anger out on Nepherian?

"Yes," Benjamin said cautiously. "But not for conversation, and the visuals will only kick in if something causes a disturbance." There Despite his exhaustion, Benjamin fortified himself for another stoush between the women. Why else would Lydia hold Nepherian back? "What don't you want overheard?" he asked Lydia.

Nepherian, oddly enough, smiled as if she were looking forward to the argument.

Benjamin began to feel like an unarmed referee in a gunfight. "Please, not tonight," he said tiredly. "Your problems can wait until tomorrow."

"No Ben," Lydia whispered. "We have to resolve this now." She glared at Nepherian with genuine anger. "This better work or I'll kill you," she said with dangerous calm, and Ben had the feeling she meant it. She turned and walked into their bedroom, closing the door and leaving Ben alone with his media advisor.

What? Now he felt even more uncomfortable. "*We* have to resolve… what?" Benjamin asked, thoroughly confused now. "I don't know what this is about Nepherian, but you need to sort it out with Lydia, not me."

Hesitantly, Nepherian moved closer. Too close. He fought the urge to step back as she invaded his personal space and remained there.

"Do you trust Lydia?" Nepherian asked softly, her skin almost too pale under the room's lights.

He really wasn't in the mood for whatever issue they had, and Nepherian was still far too close to him. "What's this about Nepherian?" he asked tersely.

"This is about Lydia doing the right thing. Finally." She sighed as if she'd just released something she wished she hadn't. She clenched her fists and seemed overly nervous now, hesitant, and it was at odds with how close she stood to him.

He attempted to divert the conversation. "I should thank you Nepherian. The voice projector caught the shot. The dart was laced with concentrated biogerm residue."

She met his eyes, studying. "Ben, do you trust Lydia? I mean really trust her – with your life?"

A cold feeling came over him, yet he couldn't quite say why. "Nepherian-"

"Ben, please. This is very important. Do you trust Lydia with your life?"

At a complete loss, he nodded. "Of course I do. Why?"

"You're a good man, Ben. The best. I wouldn't have worked for you otherwise." Her face was slightly upturned as she snuck her arms around his neck.

Alarmed, he reached for her hands."Nepherian, please. I'm your boss." That, and all Lydia had to do was walk out and he'd be in more trouble than he could dig himself out of.

As he grasped her wrists to pull them free, she drew him into kiss. Shocked, he broke her hold and stepped back, pressing the back of his hand to his mouth. She tasted like peaches. Startled and more than a little angry, he pointed to the door. "You need to leave. Now."

"I'm truly sorry," she said softly, and without any further comment she left the room, leaving him thoroughly confused. He hesitated before entering his bedroom to confront Lydia, suspecting she knew what had just happened. Why leave them alone otherwise? Why allow it? There was something going on between the two women, but he had no idea what it was. Was Lydia testing him? Testing their marriage?

"Nepherian just kissed me," he said, watching her face.

Lydia lay between the sheets of their bed, her shoulders bare. She pursed her lips as if she couldn't help her distaste at the news, but she showed absolutely no surprise. "Did you enjoy it?" she asked, one eyebrow raised.

What the hell had he missed between them? Lydia had clearly known Nepherian was going to kiss him, he was sure of it. "No," he answered honestly, his suspicions aroused. "What's going on Lydia?"

She pulled the sheets back, displaying her toned, naked body. "Make love to me honey. I'll explain it all tomorrow."

Make love? After she'd orchestrated for his media advisor to kiss him? "What's going on?" There was no compromise in his tone.

She sighed, letting him have his way. "This is about biogerm Ben."

Biogerm? What did Nepherian's kiss have to do with biogerm... A sudden fear filled him. Was Nepherian infected? Peaches. She'd tasted like peaches. He'd read something about biogerm and the taste of peaches. Worse, the silver strain was primarily passed on through saliva. The cold feeling he'd experienced earlier returned. "What have you done?" he asked Lydia.

Lydia bit her lip. "Nepherian just gave you the silver strain of biogerm."

There was fear in her eyes now, and she was right to fear. "And now you want to make love?" If she knew Nepherian was infected, and didn't fear kissing him now, that had to mean she was infected too, which made no sense whatsoever.

He tried to make sense of it. "Today's arguments to use a resonance field, to record the speech? What are you playing at? Was it all a ruse? Why? Why bring Nepherian into it? The assassin?"

She looked away. "Failed. As intended. We needed the dart to hit the voice projector. You had to be cleared of biogerm infection before we could act, the most rigorous tests. We couldn't risk anything less."

We? Her, Nepherian, who else? The dead assassin? "Why are you doing this?"

She smiled as if to assure him everything was okay. "Because no one will suspect you now."

He fought down rage and the feeling of betrayal. "Suspect? Suspect what?" He touched his lips. Peaches still.

He should be calling for his guards to have Lydia and Nepherian arrested. Yet she didn't appear afraid. More... concerned about how he'd take the news. She had more riding on this than her own safety then. What was the game? He realised his hands were shaking and crossed his arms across his chest to hide it. "Is this about the rumours of a cure?" Why else would she do it? Did she believe them?

"Ben, you said you trusted me. Do you?"

How had she heard Nepherian ask that? "I did before you conspired to infect me with an incurable alien disease," he said angrily. "Is this some sort of protest?"

"This isn't about a cure, Ben. Nepherian hosts both strains, and has for nearly a decade. She's not sick."

That caught him off guard. "What?" She should be dead. Long

dead. The survival rate for a single strain was barely more than a few years. A decade was unheard of.

"I host both strains too," Lydia whispered.

He gaped, for a long moment unable to speak. "You're both infected?" he whispered. None of it was possible. It would have been picked up in any number of medical tests.

"I'm not sick, Ben, and neither is Nepherian. We never will be. That's how biogerm works. You need both strains to form symbiosis, and once you do…" A smile formed at the corners of her mouth, but then it disappeared, replaced by sadness. "Hundreds of thousands of people have died, many murdered, to prevent that knowledge from spreading. You're the Federation's President, the only person with enough power to make a difference."

"You've killed me."

She rolled her eyes as if dealing with an upset toddler. "Symbiosis requires strains from separate hosts. Do you understand what I'm saying?"

Separate hosts? He pursed his lips, the memory of Nepherian's kiss still there.

"We have to finish this Ben. Now. You have to reach symbiosis by dawn. We can't let them know you're with us."

Fury flushed his vision and he struggled to see past it. "I'm *not* with you!"

"Shhh! You'll activate the monitors."

"Maybe I want to activate the monitors!"

She reached out with her right hand as if to placate him, but slowly let it fall. "I know I've shaken your trust, but-"

"Shaken? You've destroyed it." He needed to… what? Call security, for a start.

He stiffened as she reached under her pillow, fearing a weapon, but she only pulled out a small vial of a yellowish liquid. "Drink this then. It's derived from a natural Ophelian resin. If taken before biogerm begins invading your cells, within an hour of infection, it will neutralise it. It's the closest thing to a cure."

He stared at the vial. "I've never heard of a cure, even a time-limited one."

"For a reason! The government gives pharmaceutical companies trillions of credits for research and development, and they earn trillions more by treating the so-called disease. They buried knowledge about the resin just as they buried knowledge about symbiosis."

He shook his head in denial. "I'm the President. If that were true I'd have heard about it." He needed to sort this out, even if that meant compromising his marriage and everything else he valued. "I'm calling security."

"Ben, please don't. You need to trust me."

He took a long, angry breath, letting it out slowly. Need? "You just told me you conspired to infect me with biogerm, a death sentence, and now you're telling me there's a cure and a conspiracy, and it's all about money?"

"If you call security I'll be killed, Ben. I risked everything to bring you into this."

"Maybe you should have discussed it before infecting me!"

She held up the vial. "I am asking. Here. Now. Take it. Drink it if you want." She held it out. As he hesitantly reached for the vial she spoke again. "They'll kill Sarah too, Ben. She was infected before me."

He felt like he'd been slapped. "Sarah?" he whispered. "Tell me you haven't brought our daughter into this."

She shook her head slowly. "Sarah bought me into it, long before you were President. She achieved symbiosis eight years ago. That's why she hasn't delivered any of her babies – they'll have a natural immunity to biogerm until they reach maturity, and that can be detected in a simple blood test. You need to make it safe for her to have children Ben. Please, do this for Sarah."

He needed to sit. He'd do anything for his daughter. "Sarah," he whispered. "How?"

"Nepherian did it. She's been planning this for almost two decades. She didn't give Sarah a choice. Now you know why I hate her so much."

Lydia stood and caught his hands, wrapping his fingers around the vial of resin. "I'm giving you a choice, Ben. Take it or don't, but I swear that despite everything Nepherian did, I'd go out and get infected again if someone cured me today."

His mouth was growing dry, one of the first signs of biogerm infection. "Why?"

"Because I can feel your emotions. I can read your surface thoughts. I know I can trust you. Until a few minutes ago, you trusted me. The problem is, others can read your surface thoughts too. It's why I couldn't discuss it with you. I had to make sure everyone knew you were free of the disease. Uncompromised. If we'd discussed it you wouldn't be able to hide the knowledge, and there are people we come into contact with who know the truth. You need to be able to screen your thoughts and hide your gifts, and you needed to be above suspicion."

"You should have told me anyway," he said.

Her hands were warm around his. Soft. Gentle. "If that's your answer then I have to leave. You won't see me or Sarah again, or Nepherian. They'll kill us, Ben. Until we can expose them and ensure everyone knows the truth about biogerm, we're in danger. They influence the media, the police, and far too many people in the government. Even your position as President won't protect us for long. You have to expose the corruption, and you can't do that in ignorance."

He couldn't contain his anger. His hurt. His sense of betrayal. He childishly wanted to hurt her just as much as he felt hurt. "I don't have to do anything," he said coldly.

She dropped her eyes, sad, but not fearful. "I'm so sorry, but I did what I believed was right. At least now you know the truth. Drink the resin, Ben. It tastes horrid, but it works. Goodbye."

He caught her hands as she began to let go. Could he really let her and Sarah walk out of his life? "What happens if I achieve this symbiosis?"

"I'll stay, of course. Sarah too. Symbiosis will give you gifts as well. Amazing gifts. It's worth it. I promise."

He tried to consider all the implications, but in the end he realised he couldn't push Sarah out of his life. Despite the resentment he felt, he didn't want to lose Lydia either. Fighting off the feelings of betrayal, he said, "Do it to me then."

She watched his eyes for a long moment before cupping his face between her hands. "You'll have to make love to me. The gold strain is sexually transmitted and I couldn't risk bringing an injectable sample through security."

"I'm doing this for Sarah," he whispered, trying to make himself believe it was the only reason, though it wasn't. Not really. He was doing it for Lydia too. Everything he'd ever done was for her.

She watched his eyes, and he could see she knew the truth. "We can make a difference Ben. A real difference. We can make everything better for everyone."

Afterward

The President's Assassin is a loose sequel to Merrie Dawn. I struggled with half a dozen drafts before arriving at this version, and if I had the time I'm probably keep playing with it. Mind you, I could say that about everything I write. It's difficult to know when something's done.

The President's Assassin began life with Terrence in the role of the assassin trying to outwit corrupt authorities and expose the situation about biogerm.

Over many drafts it morphed into what it is now, and has been written from several different points of view at different times, including Lydia's. While I really loved Lydia's POV, the story began to morph into a novel, so I had to simplify it. That's when it became Ben's story.

WYVERN'S BLOOD

A VEIL OF GODS SHORT STORY: NOTE, CONTAINS GRAPHIC CONTENT AND ADULT THEMES

CHRIS ANDREWS

Ellie frowned, calculating as the izzat, disguised as a young man, laughed at a jest from a drunken human girl.

As the izzat stepped back she moved forward and bumped into him, spilling half of her scotch and coke.

"Watch out you moron," she said in a slight accent over the sounds of the thumping dance music. She moved the drink between hands and shook the wet one, then dried it on her faded blue jeans.

Half-drunk, the izzat turned and sneered down at her, "Watch it yourself!" he said, glancing at her unusual white hair. "What happened to you? See a ghost?"

She glared. "A wyvern, actually." She glanced at his watch. "Nice projector. Creates a first-class illusion. Amazing what technology can do."

His expression turned hard as he unconsciously covered the device on his wrist. "Who are you?"

She walked past him, finding an empty table on the far side of the room. She placed her drink on a wet coaster and glanced out the window at a street lit by overhead lights and busy with cars. From the corner of her eye she watched the izzat cross the room and drop his lean frame on the bench opposite her.

"Who are you?" he said coldly. He leaned on the heavy wooden table, his expression dangerous.

Ellie took a sip of her drink and placed it back on the wet coaster. "So, what's a non-human doing on a human world?"

He frowned, hesitating. "Exploratory team. We're considering initiating contact. How did you detect my disguise?" He didn't seem nearly so drunk as before.

She smiled. "I can see the energy field it projects."

His eyes leveled on hers. "You're not human either, are you?"

She glanced out the window again. "I was. Another world. Another universe." She presented her hand to him for inspection. He took it. "Watch out for the tips of my fingers. Put enough pressure on them and claws stick out. Very sharp."

He raised his eyebrows as he cautiously held her hand up to the dim light. "You've got scales! Gods, they're so fine they look like skin." He released her hand and gave her a calculated smile probably supposed to put her at ease. "Want to tell me about it? I'm Garris, by the way. Gary here."

"Ellie," she said. "As I mentioned, I had a run-in with a wyvern. Got infected with wyvern's blood."

He raised an eyebrow. "I didn't think dragon-kind remained in this world."

Did she detect a hint of concern? She downed the remaining half of her drink and put the glass back on the table. "You're right. They don't exist here." She waited a moment before continuing. "Listen, I'm sorry I was rude to you. I got irritated when I spilled my drink," she lied. "I need another. Can I get you a beer? Make up for it?"

He sat back on the bench. "Yeah. Sure. I'll get the next round."

She smiled. "Deal." She left, returning a few minutes later with a beer for him and a scotch and coke for herself.

"So," he said, "What's your story? Tell me everything." He took a sip of his beer and frowned. He held it up, a question on his face.

"Extra bitter," she said. "Sorry, I should have asked."

"It'll do."

She rested the back of her head against the wall. "Been a long time since I've really spoken to anyone about it." She let longing touch her features, quickly smothered. "By the Creator, far too long. How much time you got?"

He glanced at his dual-purpose watch. "Till dawn. Then I turn into a gutter drunk." He laughed, though it sounded forced to Ellie.

She played along, producing a smile. "So you're the reason they close early here? As I said, another world, another universe. It began the year our village had to choose a sacrifice for the wyvern. He came every seven years and took a virgin girl." She pushed a few strands of loose white hair from her face. "I was sixteen. The lands were wild back then, and probably still are. My father, the local blacksmith, wasn't a particularly well-liked man. Lazy. A bully. Bit of a cheat. I adored him and he me. My mother I don't remember. She died from disease when I was young." Her lips pursed in bitter memory. "I had brown hair, like her." She closed her eyes, remembering as…

…Trestal, the village elder, called out a name. Ellie recognised it as her own, but it made no sense. A cold spring breeze tussled her hair and sent a shiver into her lower back. Goosebumps prickled her skin. She should have worn a warmer dress.

"No!" her father yelled from behind, making her jump in surprise. He wrapped his thick arms around her, drawing her to him. "She's my only child! Choose another."

"The draw was fair, Meham," Trestal called from the wooden platform. "You watched."

"You're not taking her. Anyone here tries to touch her and I'll-"

Ellie heard a dull whack, and then her father fell, taking her with him to the muddy ground. "No!" she screamed as two men pulled her away from her father. She cried out and struggled uselessly as they hauled her from the square, their fingers bruising her arms.

Trestal followed as they dragged her down the muddy street and away from the crowd. Beyond the edge of the village they lashed her wrists together around a stout pole, and then left her there as tears crossed her cheeks.

"I'm sorry," Trestal called as he walked away. He glanced upward and a look of concern and fear crossed his face. He swore, but the wind carried his words away. He hurried back to the relative safety of the village.

She followed his gaze and saw the gold underside of the wyvern as he glided toward her on the breeze. "Lords of the Higher Realm, save me!" she cried.

She struggled with the cords binding her wrists but they only bit deeper, chafing her skin. Her vision blurred with tears. She pulled until her wrists bled and the wyvern landed heavily behind her, his claws biting into the wet earth.

Heat radiated from the wyvern like a forge. She risked a glance back and cried out.

At the withers he stood taller than a barn, his lean muscles hard.

He folded his green-scaled wings, leaving only his chest and inner legs showing gold. His long tail flicked through the air, the golden underside quickly coming to rest against the muddy earth. His yellow eyes regarded her only briefly before he took her in a claw and lifted her up over the pole.

Ellie cried out as he sprang into the air, but his grip was surprisingly gentle. She pulled the cord binding her wrists loose with her teeth, then struggled and kicked as he held her close. He showed no signs he even felt her.

His wings caught an up-draught and stopped beating as he turned into a smooth glide. She thumped her fists against his claw, trying to force him to drop her – better that than any death he might have for her, but he turned her in his grip and she felt him shift.

Suddenly he was only twice her size.

She screamed as both his forearms wrapped around her. Rushing air carried her cries away as his rear claws took hold of her legs. All her struggling couldn't have prevented what happened next.

Something scalding hot entered her.

Ellie cried out in shock and pain as the burning spread through her. She blacked out in fear and pain, only to wake and cry out once more when the wyvern withdrew from her.

Hot liquid stung her thighs but she lay unmoving, listless and staring at nothing, a dull ache in her stomach.

Ellie barely noticed as the wyvern shifted back to his natural size. Pain, humiliation and fear buried her thoughts deep.

She lost consciousness long before a cave closed around them, waking on cold stone to an icy draft and an aching stomach. Darkness pressed in on her and stars revealed themselves beyond the wide entrance.

The wyvern remained unseen, but she felt his presence pressing against her mind. She turned her head and closed her eyes in revulsion.

Exhaustion claimed her once more. Reflected daylight from the entrance eventually woke her. Exhausted and hot, she blinked hard before the cavern came into focus.

Crouched on all fours beside the entrance, his long tail wrapped around his talons, the wyvern watched her. His presence still thick against her mind, Ellie turned away as much with fear as disgust with herself.

She felt sick in the stomach, but it took a moment to realise the reason. Her belly was swollen, the wool of her dress tight. She moved and felt an ache deep inside.

"Gods of the Higher Realm." She glared fearfully at the wyvern as she placed a hand on her swollen belly. "What did you do to me?"

The wyvern raised his head slightly. His ears stood up above short, rear-pointing horns.

"Our females have no womb to carry fertilised eggs. It falls to the male to take the eggs and find a surrogate," he said in a surprisingly soft, deep voice. "The greater dragons once carried our eggs for us, though they are few in this world since the female unicorn was slain. With only one unicorn remaining, there isn't enough natural magic in the world to sustain more than a few of the greater dragons. Fortunately your kind are able to grow healthy eggs, and your flesh is nourishing to the drakes."

The implications closed around her like chains. She swallowed the acid that rose with the fear in her throat. "You mean I'm going to lay eggs, and when they hatch they're going to eat me?"

"Of course." He sounded as if she should already know that. "The draken," at her confused expression, he said, "The greater dragons, carried our eggs full size for us, where you cannot. The drakes will hatch small and require your flesh as sustenance for the first few weeks after hatching."

Her breath frosted in the cold air, though she didn't feel the cold other than on her skin. She tried to stand, but there was no strength in her legs and she collapsed back to the stone.

She stared back at the wyvern in horror. "I hate you," she said. His presence against her mind smothered her like the haystack that had once fallen on her as a child. She felt short of breath.

Massive shoulders flexed as he stood on all fours, his head scant yards from the cavern's roof. "You knew your fate when I came for you."

"I only knew fear!" She forced her weak arms to push her into a sitting position, though the effort cost her more than she felt she had. "My people know only fear! Why do you think they had to tie me to a post?"

His nostrils flared over his narrow, toothy muzzle. "A bargain is a bargain. Your people prosper under my protection."

"They'd rather be free!"

"So would I!" he roared.

Ellie rested her back against the wall. "You're a parasite," she whispered. Her eyes closed. She was so tired she couldn't keep them open. She could feel the heat in her body burning up her strength. "If I had a weapon I'd kill myself."

"And I would be forced to destroy your village."

With the last of her strength she said, "After what they did to me, do you think I care?" With that she collapsed into unconsciousness.

His presence haunted her sleep like a weight around her soul, keeping her restless and her sleep fitful. She woke to an agony of stomach cramps in pitch darkness, her dress already torn at the seams.

The wyvern stirred at her movement, but she couldn't see him. Between cramps she managed to pull her dress over her head and use it as a pillow. By dawn she felt so hot she had to keep crawling around the floor to find cool stone, despite the icy draft.

As the first touch of sun found the cave, she screamed in agony.

A dozen soft-shelled eggs spilled from between her legs amid a slick of blood and clear acrid fluid. She crawled a few yards away and collapsed, not caring that the uneven stone bit into her aching belly. She lay there until the sun reached its peak before finding the strength to move again, her only thought to get away from the eggs before the drakes hatched and found her.

She managed to drag herself a dozen feet before collapsing, her energy expended, though the heat of her body could have rivaled a small campfire.

Dusk settled before she felt strong enough to move again. In near darkness the wyvern regarded her from his position near the entrance, its presence a sentinel against her escape.

She swallowed in a dry throat and said, "Why don't you just kill me?"

His ears stood up. "Your flesh must be fresh for the drakes."

"I hate you." She pushed herself up on her elbow, resting there a moment. "Why am I so tired?"

The wyvern regarded her with his head cocked to one side.

"What happened to me when you raped me?"

"Not rape," the wyvern said, as if finally understanding. "As per our covenant, you carried my mate's eggs for her. The eggs lay in birth fluid which becomes a part of you if it doesn't kill you first. The fluid makes your body hot enough to nurture the eggs. It also makes dragon blood flow in your veins. The blood makes more birth fluid and the fluid nurtures you for as long as you carry the eggs."

"Makes me part wyvern?" She laughed sourly at the irony. "Are wyverns cannibals now?"

He lifted his head and looked down his snout at her. "You are not of dragon kind. Even should I let you leave, you would only survive a few months. Dragon blood is in you. It will destroy you now the eggs are birthed."

She closed her eyes, resting her head against the cool stone. "So I'll die no matter what happens?"

The wyvern inclined his head.

A sickening feeling almost choked her. She took a deep breath and asked, "When will the eggs hatch?"

"The shells should harden by morning. They will hatch shortly after that."

She was quiet for a while, her stomach twisting with fear and anger, but strangely no hunger. Tiredness overwhelmed her.

She awoke with a start as the wyvern's normally calm presence against her mind reacted to danger. Dawn's light lit the cave, the sounds of heavy breathing coming from without. She glanced at the eggs. The silvery shells looked hard.

The wyvern's ears twitched, but he didn't look at her. He watched the entrance. A few moments later Ellie heard the sound of a bow release and saw an arrow strike the wyvern's muzzle and deflect harmlessly to the ground.

The wyvern's nostrils flared as he turned his head. "Village man," he said, his breath nearly as hot as fire. "If we have a quarrel I do not know of it."

"Give me back my daughter and we have no quarrel."

"Father!" Ellie cried. Hope surged.

Another arrow deflected harmlessly off the wyvern's scales. The wyvern stood. "Leave now!" he roared. The air wavered with the heat in his breath.

Her father stepped into the cave entrance. "Let me see my daughter!"

The wyvern's long tail whipped through the air, striking stone from the wall behind him. Something rumbled deep in his chest and his ears stood forward. "I understand your anguish, village man. Leave your weapons where you stand and you may enter."

"I don't trust you. I'll keep my weapons."

The wyvern roared, the sound nearly shattering Ellie's hearing. She covered her ears with her hands, crying out and shedding a tear with the pain. She could feel the wyvern's anger when he spoke again. "I could obliterate you where you stand, village man. Your weapons are useless. I will not make my offer again."

Meham cursed, but dropped his bow and quiver. The wyvern moved to allow him entrance, and when he saw Ellie he ran. She cried with too many emotions as he knelt before her and pulled her close.

"You're burning up," he said. "By the Higher Realm you're hot!" He glared at the wyvern. "She's sick. You must let me take her home."

"She will soon be dead. Her sacrifice will feed the drakes."

Meham swore under his breath. Aloud, he said, "You'll have to kill me before I'd allow that to happen."

The sound of a shell cracking interrupted them. Ellie glanced at the eggs. "They're hatching, father. Please leave. You can't save me."

"Never." He pulled a dagger from his belt. "I'll kill the drakes first."

He took two steps toward the eggs but a burst of flame washed over Ellie and struck him. He screamed as his clothing and hair burst into flame and his dagger tumbled to the stone.

"Father!" Ellie cried.

He screamed louder as he tried to put the flames out, stumbling wildly as he tore his cloak and shirt from his body. He staggered closer to the eggs as another burst of flame struck him. He finally fell to the ground with an agonised cry.

He thrashed against the stone for long seconds before a groan passed his lips and he lay still. The flames died on his blackened body and the nauseating stench of burnt flesh filled the air.

"I'll kill you!" Ellie yelled impotently at the wyvern. "I'll kill you and all your kind!"

The wyvern glared back. "Your father broke our covenant. Be thankful I do not seek revenge on your people."

The first drake broke from its shell.

Green skinned, it craned its long neck and made a high-pitched call, quickly answered by muffled replies from the other eggs. Ellie cried out, pushing herself away.

Shaking as much from weakness as fear, her endurance gave out. She closed her eyes and buried her head under her arms to wait for the inevitable. Another egg cracked, and in quick succession two more.

Tears broke from her closed eyes and she sobbed loudly enough that she didn't hear the excited calls of the first drake as it found her father's body. It wasn't until more hatched that she realised what was happening. She lifted her head and glared at them with all the hatred inside her.

"Get away from him!" she yelled. "Leave him alone!" They ignored her. Too weak to move any further, she buried her face in her arms to be tortured by the sounds of their feast.

When they were done the drakes flew from the cave in a small cloud, leaving her alone with their sire and the bloody remains of her father's body. The wyvern stretched his legs.

"Are you going to eat me?" she asked. She pushed herself to her knees with an effort.

The wyvern laughed at her, the sound deep and echoing. "Only our first meal is flesh, and only then if we hatch small. We are creatures of magic."

"Then what's to happen to me?"

"You will die slowly. The blood in your veins will destroy your body without the birth fluid in your womb to nurture you. It will not be pleasant."

"Then kill me. My father is gone and I won't return to my people. Kill me. Quickly."

The wyvern raised his ears. "You do not wish to live a few more months?"

"For what?" she said bitterly. "Kill me. Please. I beg you."

"As you wish."

He took a deep breath and fire washed over her like a warm blanket. Her nearby dress burned away in an instant, but when the heat passed she remained untouched.

He frowned. "Strange." He took another breath, and pure fire warped the air with heat, stinging her skin.

Flame flashed throughout the cavern, cremating the bloody bones of her father and blackening the silvery shells left by the drakes. When it was over, her knees rested on rock glowing red from the heat.

Her skin was almost a silvery colour. "Kill me!" she cried. "I don't want to die slowly."

The dragon snarled, revealing huge teeth. She felt his irritation.

His next breath struck and she cried out in agony. Flame seared into her and through her, burning away everything that remained human inside her. When it eased, she found herself kneeling in six inches of molten rock, its heat an enjoyable warmth compared to the wyvern's breath.

"No!" the wyvern roared, its sudden unexplained fear palpable against her mind. Another burst of flame slapped her backwards to the cavern wall, melting the stone behind her. She writhed and screamed in pain until the wyvern's breath stopped.

Slowly, as if new to movement, she took a deep breath and stood, wiping molten stone from her body. Fine bronze scales covered her skin and her hair had gone white. She stared at her hands as if they were someone else's, and then looked up at the wyvern.

"What have you done to me?" she asked in a voice she didn't recognise. His eyes reflected the shock and fear she felt from him in her mind.

"No!" he roared loud enough to have shattered her eardrums only minutes before. He sprang at her, a huge claw smashing her across the cavern.

She crashed into the wall and fell to the floor, a shower of fine stone dusting her. Shaken but unhurt, she carefully stood. A slapped cheek a day ago would have stung more. She stared at her limbs in wonder.

She could almost touch the wyvern's fear. She reached out without knowing quite how and twisted something. He screamed in pain.

Sudden realisation struck her harder than the wyvern's blow. She almost sank to her knees. She knew his *Name*. It was now part of her own. He was hers to command.

"Get out of here," she said, testing.

The wyvern bolted for the entrance and sprang into the air with a roar of rage. With a snap of his wings he was gone.

She followed him to the entrance and stared in wonder while cool air caressed her new bronze scales. With perfect vision she watched the wyvern fly as fast as he could toward the far ranges.

The leaves of trees on distant mountains were individually visible to her, and she felt the natural magics in the air.

She too, was now a creature of magic.

She knelt, touching the stone and feeling the elemental fire deep within the earth, and the magic that bound it there.

She jumped from the edge of the cavern and landed lightly more than two hundred feet below as if skipping down steps. Her mind echoed with the emotions and unguarded thoughts of hundreds of wyvern across the world, and through them discovered other girls dying as she almost had.

Anger suffused her thoughts as she walked among spring wild-flowers. She breathed in the fresh mountain air, feeling the currents of natural magic about her as a normal person would wind.

The cold hardly touched her as she made her way back to the village. She walked through an entire night and the following day and only stopped at the Mendder's farm to steal a dress of dark blue from their eldest daughter's room.

The coarse wool slipped easily across her fine-scaled flesh.

Farmers she knew watched her pass without recognition, more curious about her white hair than anything else.

On the second evening she arrived at her village, sustained by the world's natural magics.

She ignored the curious stares from familiar faces and made her way to her father's forge. Inside she found a polished steel mirror.

Someone she didn't know stared back. Even her eyes had lost some of their natural deep brown and were now tinged with yellow around the pupils.

She put on a leather apron to protect her dress and fired up the forge with enough fuel to make a hardened blacksmith curse and back away.

While it heated she collected the mirror and every other scrap of steel in the workshop, placing it all in the coals. She stroked the elemental magic in the fire, caressing it like a lover.

When glowing she pulled two pieces of steel from the fire with her hands. She thought of the wyvern and her anger swelled, the soft steel bending in her grip. She pounded the two pieces with a hefty hammer, folding them together over the anvil and binding the elemental fire magic into the steel.

The door creaked open to reveal Trestal's slim form.

"What do you want, Trestal?" she asked before he could set a foot inside.

He raised his white eyebrows, peering at her suspiciously. "Who are you?"

She returned the still-hot metal to the forge. "Surely you

remember a girl you sentenced to death only a few days ago?" Though she tried she couldn't keep the bitterness from her voice.

The old man's jaw dropped. "Ellie?" He stepped over the threshold, staring at her with a deep frown and squint. "By the Gods!"

She reached into the fire with a bare hand and pulled the glowing blade of a sickle out, then a damaged rim from someone's cart. Trestal stared at her in shock. Without the benefit of the anvil she twisted them together then threw them back to the heat. "What do you want, Trestal?"

His eyes moved from the forge to her as she began pumping the bellows. "What are you doing?" He leaned against the doorframe as if uncertain he could stand on his own.

"Forging a spear." She pulled a couple of horseshoes from the glowing coals and bent them around each other.

"But-"

"Trestal! My father is dead and I wish I were. I don't blame you for what happened to me, but I'm going to make sure this never happens again. Unless you wish to help, get out."

He watched her pull more glowing metal from the fire with her bare hands. "I'll pass the word you're to be left alone," he said. With an unsteady nod he turned and left.

For hours she labored at the forge, folding steel into a huge lump even a blacksmith would be hard pressed to lift. When done she placed it back into the coals and closed her eyes, sensing the magical properties of the fire.

With her new awareness she forced the escaping elemental magic back into the forge, melding the fire and steel together like an alloy. When hot enough to trigger a resonant response, she called to the earth and heat deep within answered.

Hoping she wasn't violating some sacred principle of magic, she built a link between the steel and the heat below. When she opened her eyes she found steel the colour of the sun, its form unchanged. She pulled it from the forge, scalding even her hands. For long hours she shaped it, re-heating it regularly with the earth's elemental magic until she had a spear ten-foot long and as thick as her wrist.

Still glowing, she took it outside where it made sunlight seem dim, and threw shadows behind people and objects. Villagers she knew squinted at her as she passed them, shying away.

"Ellie?" one matron called.

Ellie stopped briefly as she caught the woman's eye, nodded slightly, then continued on, otherwise ignoring the woman who'd once kindly given the blacksmith's child her own daughters' outgrown clothes.

At the creek she knelt and whispered, "This is for you, Father," and dropped the spear to quench in a screaming hiss of elemental agony.

Steam billowed into the air, submersing her for minutes in a white fog rising above the willows. When the creek boiled dry she took the dark spear and silently called, commanding the wyvern's presence.

A roar of rage sounded deep in her mind, shackled by her mastery of his Name.

In a blast of hatred she sensed the wyvern spring into the sky. He resisted her demands like an eel would a man's grip, but she forced him forward despite his efforts to turn away. Hours passed as she waited, the wyvern using every stray breeze to delay his arrival.

She watched as he finally came into view, her own hatred coursing inside her. The moment arrived. She gripped her cold spear and moved to face him.

The wyvern landed before her, fear in his eyes as she hefted her magic-wrought spear. He remained standing as if her mastery of his Name could change at any moment and he might achieve freedom from her.

An unspoken command forced him to drop to his belly.

"Kill me then," he said. "It will change nothing."

"Oh, you're right," she said as she approached his chest, close to his heart. She touched the point of her spear to his scales and ran it down his side without leaving a mark. "But I'm not going to kill you. I'm going to make you suffer. You're going to help me kill all of your kind, and then you're going to live with it. I'm going to make sure this never happens to another girl again."

The wyvern's howl of ineffective rage reached the mountains as she sprang to his back and commanded him to fly…

…Ellie opened her eyes to the dim nightclub, her heart still beating hard with remembered emotion.

"What happened then?" the izzat asked. He hadn't taken his eyes from her.

Ellie glanced at him. "I spent the next ten years hunting wyverns," she said. Her expression turned inward again. "I wasn't very good at it, actually. Only injured two. Most refused to fight – kept flying away. They're not stupid, at least not the old ones. The seventh one killed my mount when we caught him by surprise. A fall of a thousand feet knocks the wind out of you – in case you've never tried it. If it hadn't been for my spear he would have killed me, too."

"He killed your mount? You mean the wyvern who's Name you knew?"

She nodded. "Actually, I think he suicided. Didn't put up much of a fight, anyhow."

"What did you do then?"

"I didn't know any of their Names, so I couldn't command any, but I could track them by their emotions and thoughts. Travelling on foot took time though, and it was nearly two years before I cornered a small female in a cave her mate had once used to hatch their young."

"So you killed her?" he asked, a hint of a smile implying approval.

Her index finger pressed against the table and a sharp claw protruded, revealing a trace of dried blood on it. She frowned, releasing the pressure. "No," she said as the claw disappeared.

His smile dissolved as he leaned forward. "Why not?"

Her lips barely held off a sneer. "I only thought I'd trapped her. She'd actually trapped me. There were two more outside. Big males. Together they could have torn me apart. Instead she offered me a deal."

His eyes widened. "You dealt with them? Gods. Dragonkind are the most dangerous and cunning creatures my people have ever discovered. We avoid them. Always."

She shrugged. "Didn't have much choice, remember? It was deal or die. The deal was this; they would never use another girl as a surrogate again if I promised to give up my crusade and leave them in peace. I had the feeling they didn't want this to happen again any more than I did. I think they even felt sorry for me."

"Doesn't explain how you got here."

"When I gave them my spear they taught me to travel between worlds – to get rid of me no doubt. I used to think I got the better deal. I'm not so sure now."

"I'm curious. How do they, you know, reproduce without using girls as surrogates?" he asked.

She shrugged. "I didn't stay to find out. I guess they use cattle or something."

He screwed his face up. "Oh. Sorry I asked."

"They've gotta do something, I suppose. How about we change the subject?"

"Fine by me. So, why'd you came to Earth? It's pretty backward."

She laughed. "Compared to what? I crossed the veil between my universe and yours about two hundred years ago. Almost every world I visited before here was either colonised, lifeless, or destroyed by war, all resources taken."

He sat up straighter, his expression closed. "And?"

"And then I found a world not far from here. Primitive people, lovely world. It was a paradise. Strangely enough, a bunch of izzen surveyed the place then wiped the people there out, despite my efforts to negotiate. They raped the world. Took everything."

Any friendliness he'd shown disappeared. "So you know why I'm here then."

She downed her drink. He'd finished his already. "Yeah." She gave him a pointed look. "Did I mention I killed your other team member this afternoon? No? Sorry, must have slipped my mind."

He stared in shock. "You bitch!" he whispered under his breath. He reached for a small laser cutter at his belt, but found it gone.

She held it up and showed it to him before crushing it in her hand. "This is my home now. You're not going to destroy it."

He sat back, a sneer on his lips. "You're too late. I've made my survey. I'll be returning home as soon as I get to my ship."

She smiled. "Really. Did you enjoy your beer?"

"What?"

"Your beer? Did you enjoy it? Wasn't it a little bitter?"

He swallowed. Hard. "What did you do?"

She held up a finger and forced the claw out. It still had a hint of her dried blood on it. "Just added a little dragon blood, that's all. Oh, don't stand up, you'll puke. That's why I told you my story - keep you seated while your stomach had time to absorb the blood. Mouth feel dry yet? Getting tired?"

He looked worried. "Maybe."

She blew him a kiss. "Enjoy the rest of your life."

"You mean I've got months?" Relief crossed his face. "I can get home and find a cure by then, easily. Cryosleep and FTL travel. Did I mention that? I might arrive home decades from now, but to me it'll be moments." He laughed.

"I put blood in your beer, not an egg in your gut. In about an hour you'll be a red slick on the pavement."

He paled. "Wait. I can-"

She stood up, leaning forward with both hands on the table. "What? Bullshit your way out of this? Not a chance, izzat. Gotta go call the media. There's a ship that needs to be discovered. I've studied your people too, by the way. I plan on sharing what I know." She patted him on the cheek. "By the time the next survey ship arrives, this world will be expecting it. It'll be hundreds of years before your people figure out something's gone wrong."

"But—"

She held up her hand, forestalling anything else. "When the wyverns realised they'd made a mistake, they fixed it. Your people are going to find out they've made an even bigger one. Let's see what they learn."

Afterward

Wyvern's Blood was the very first short story I wrote (outside of school) and had published.

I'd just joined the Canberra Speculative Fiction Guild, a new writers group that had decided to put an anthology together as a group project.

The anthology, Nor of Human, was very well received and put the CSFG on the map of Australian speculative fiction communities.

The concept for the story came from watching nature documentaries, in particular wasps that stung their prey to use them as live incubators and as a fresh food supply for their young. A horrid thing to watch, yet so fascinating you can't turn away.

SILVER RAIN ON A MOONLIT NIGHT

A VEIL OF GODS SHORT STORY

Despite the agony and effort of separation, Amaranthis forced her mind beyond the four huge trunks of her tree as darkness deepened over the Australian National Botanical Gardens.

As she separated she drew some of its heartwood with her to create a new body.

Wood and bark melded with her lifeforce to form the appearance of skin and hair, a solid illusion that would even feel real to anyone who touched her.

She dropped to her knees and coughed up a dribble of stinging sap tinged with silver before wiping her mouth with a dead eucalypt leaf. Her tree wasn't an actual eucalypt, but it looked and acted like one to help them blend in.

After spitting once more, she gingerly cupped the silver-flecked sap she'd gotten rid of within a handful of detrius to ensure none of the silver touched her new body, and staggered the few steps to the concrete path. The path was also flecked with silver. Taking a deep breath as if still human, she jumped across, staggering and nearly falling to her new knees with weakness.

Mustering her strength again, she walked well beyond her tree's root system and threw the poisonous silver-laced sap as far as she could on the down slope, making sure it never washed back.

The large, orange, rising full moon illuminated the landscape as she returned to her tree and slumped to the ground just before the silver-laced path, breathing hard as if she were a human who'd just done a marathon.

The memory of her pain-filled roots, branches and leaves slowly faded from her wooden bones, leaving a dull ache she'd never be able to remove as long as her tree grew in the midst of silver filings. It wasn't the tree that was in pain. Not really. Silver didn't affect it in the same way it did her. It hurt her, threatening to sever her lifeforce and kill her. Deep underground she could feel her tree's fine roots, slowly absorbing the silver which had leeched into the soil. She put her hand against the earth and put energy into a command. "Expel," she whispered.

A silver-flecked leaf dropped to the ground an arm's length from her, its veins lined with silver. She felt slightly better for the silver being gone from her tree, but it wasn't enough. It would never be enough as long as she was trapped here.

Struggling to stand, she very carefully picked up the tainted leaf by the stem to avoid the veins of silver. It had been months since she'd had the energy to expel silver, and it had drained her meagre reserves of lifeforce. It was necessary though if she wanted to survive.

She glared at the concrete path encircling her tree, silver filings had been sprinkled into it while the concrete had been wet. They'd been strewn below it as well, and mixed into the sand and gravel under the path.

"Bastard," she muttered. Grimacing, she walked downhill as far from her tree as she could stand to go without feeling ill, maybe a couple of hundred yards, and threw the contaminated leaf into bushes so it was unlikely to be found before the leaf itself deteriorated. What tarnished silver remained wouldn't be noticed.

Glancing back, she could almost sense the silver spikes hammered into the earth and through the roots of her tree as well, making it impossible to withdraw from the contaminated ground. She could move her tree as much as a hundred yards in a night, but Finn had used the silver to keep her in place, abusing the trust and generosity she'd given him.

Hatred quickened the sap in her veins. With Aramanthis trapped, Finn was able to milk her for the lifeforce she desperately needed to thrive and protect her Gardens.

She'd saved every spare scrap of lifeforce she could over the last month, hoping to use it to escape, but it was barely more than enough to expel the dissolved silver from her tree. She'd never have enough energy to deal with it all unless...

She clenched her small fists as she looked around the drought-stricken Garden, wishing she'd seen her fate coming. He'd seemed so kind. She'd given him health and youth in exchange for his help, and stupidly asked him to carry a broken silver necklace a little girl had dropped to the bin. Once he realised what it meant to her he'd become her worst enemy. First the silver-laced spikes, and then the path.

The trees and plants she once protected were suffering from the drought, and she had no residual energy to spare for them. Whenever she could she'd been forced to draw from them instead, some giving their lives willingly. She didn't deserve it.

The grounds staff did their best to keep the plants alive, but many of the native shrubs had died already and more were likely to follow over the course of the summer. As they died she accepted their meagre lifeforce, but not before.

Letting herself die would be easier, but if she died she couldn't protect her Gardens or her tree. Yet if she lived he'd keep milking her energy.

She did a slow, distant circle of her tree, heartbroken at the struggling plants she found in the surrounds. She ran her fingertips through dying leaves, feeling their pain. Their death knells. They couldn't help her without giving up their own lives, and she couldn't help them without giving up hers.

Still, those strong enough whispered to her through soft sighs and gentle movements, begging her to take their lives so she could protect those remaining. With so much silver in the ground, she couldn't sense them unless she walked among them, her fingers touching their dry branches and dying leaves.

"I know," she whispered to a newly-planted eucalypt who offered its lifeforce as she touched its leaves. "But you're young. You could live for centuries in a place like this. Keep your strength. You'll need it this summer."

Exhausted from the short walk she made her way back and froze when she saw the silhouette of a man standing just inside the poisoned concrete path encircling her tree.

A human shape struggled on the leaf and bark litter at his feet, the figure bound and gagged. Aramanthis shivered in both desire and fear. As she got nearer she saw it was a woman, too scared to cry out around her gag. Aramanthis felt both elated and petrified, her sap quickening.

She closed her eyes, wishing the relief Finn's latest victim brought her wasn't so intense. His victim was a little overweight and in her middle years, but a human full of lifeforce regardless. The human body held far more lifeforce than the Gardens could grant Aramanthis even if she took everything and killed every plant for miles around.

Aramanthis hated herself for the desperation which made her hurry. She needed the woman's lifeforce, and the lives of humans were far less important than her garden. Using what little strength she had, she jumped the path and crouched, staring at her victim's fear-filled eyes. The woman's terrified tears left streaks of mascara down her face.

Maybe in her fifties, she tried to speak, to beg for help, but the gag garbled her voice. Aramanthis took a deep breath, smelling the lifeforce emanating from the woman as if it were warmth. It was like smelling a meal.

"I need more nectar," Finn said in his harsh, gravelly voice. With her trapped and he able to milk her for her nectar, he'd taken up smoking again, certain her nectar would always be able to heal him. He was right. "I have a buyer."

She thought of him as Bruiser because his victims almost always came bruised. He cared nothing about Aramanthis' welfare, or his victims, or that she'd soon draw the lifeforce from this woman to make his nectar.

"I'm sorry," Aramanthis whispered to the woman, fingertips brushing a tear away from a bruised cheek. The woman flinched. "You'll soon be dead."

Once, Aramanthis had had no capacity for sympathy and had killed more humans than she needed to, allowing everything around her to bloom even in the harshest conditions. Now, empathy was so ingrained in her she couldn't feel anything but sympathy.

The woman wasn't too badly hurt considering Finn had taken a steel pipe to some of his victims. Her left cheek was swollen and dark in contrast to the greying roots of her hair, but Aramanthis couldn't see any other injury. She must have gone down with one hit.

Aramanthis glanced up at Finn, then hungrily back at the woman who must have recognised something in Aramanthis, because now she struggled in earnest, whimpering and crying into her gag. Finn kicked her in the side to keep her silent.

Aramanthis gritted her teeth, trying not to react. "She's not enough," she said to Finn. "The silver is poisoning me. She'll barely keep me alive. I need at least one more to make your nectar."

"You'll make the nectar with just her or I'll take a chainsaw to your tree. It's got four trunks. Would you prefer one or two?"

She stared, shocked at the threat. It would kill them in these conditions. "But-"

"I'll collect the nectar at dawn. Get it done."

"You'll kill your golden goose," she said angrily. "I'm not strong enough."

A punch to her jaw sent her sprawling. She was so weak she hadn't even seen it coming. Almost like a human, her head pounded as she struggled to her elbows, dead leaves sticking to her arms and face. She winced as she brushed them away.

"You'll have my nectar by dawn or I'll start flicking lit matches about your precious Gardens."

Fear caught her breath. Would he really burn the Australian National Botanic Gardens? Would he risk it? Would he dare? She wasn't sure she had the courage to call him on it.

The Gardens were entirely planted with native species, and natives burned well. Some would survive, and some would use the fire to seed a new generation, but thousands would die and have to be replanted.

Still on the ground, Aramanthis glared as defiantly as her courage allowed. "Then remove some of the silver spikes," she said, hoping he'd dig up at least one or two. There was little he could do about the silver filings he'd sprinkled under the path as he'd poured the concrete, but the spikes could come out. She couldn't touch them herself and they were in too deep to simply pull out even with her hands cocooned by dead leaves, but with a pick or shovel he could.

His small landscaping business was often called in for maintenance work and small projects like new paths, and the path surrounding the tree had been one of them. He'd done it at cost, he'd told her, just for the chance to trap her properly.

"Remove the spikes and take the chance you'll escape?" His expression suggested she thought he was stupid. He wasn't, but he wasn't as smart as he thought he was.

"There's enough silver under the path to trap a dozen dryads," she said, the ache from the punch settling into her wooden jaw. With enough lifeforce she could craft a real human body, down to blood and bone, but for now she had little enough to leave her tree.

The punch would have bruised if she'd had the energy to craft a human body. Instead it would scab over like bark and probably take the rest of the summer to heal if she remained outside her tree.

"That's not a risk I'll take."

Desperate for some respite to regain some strength, she tried the only leverage she had. "And if it kills me? I've kept you young for a decade. I can keep you young forever if we work together, but you'll die if you kill me."

He frowned as if she'd just said something stupid. "There are other dryads in the world. I know the signs now. I'll find one."

She glanced at the victim he'd bought her, fearful that he might just do that. "You know nothing about us."

"I know I can use you to make money, lots of money. One sip of nectar will take years off a person or heal almost any illness. Do you know what a desperate person will pay to cure their child of cancer?"

Callous bastard. "Then you'd better drink the next nip yourself. That's a melanoma on your neck you bloody idiot." She couldn't help the spite in her voice. "And from the sound of your clogged arteries it'll be a race to see which kills you first, cancer or cholesterol."

He lost his arrogant expression, but a moment later he kicked the bound woman, eliciting a grunt of pain, followed by a low keening cry.

"Leave her alone," Aramanthis whispered. She'd been on the receiving end of enough of his kicks to know how it felt.

"Make the nectar Aramanthis or I'll burn everything within sight and well beyond." He leaned closer, whisky on his breath. "But if you're a good little dryad I'll give you a ride in my new Ferrari instead." He chuckled as if he'd actually made a joke she might appreciate. He turned and followed the moonlit path back toward the car park.

Slumping in both relief and fear, Aramanthis took a minute to push herself upright and rest her back against her tree.

She glanced at the bound woman, desperation in the human's eyes. The woman's body would nourish Aramanthis' tree, but her lifeforce would nourish Aramanthis. Normally.

If she wasn't so weak from silver poisoning she could use a little of the lifeforce to draw more silver into another leaf and discard it, and still make nectar.

She wasn't strong enough though, and she needed what little lifeforce she had to escape Finn's snare. If she could.

"I'm sorry for what I'm going to have to do," Aramanthis said. The woman lay above one of the silver spikes buried in the ground, which wouldn't work. Aramanthis got to her knees and dragged her victim closer to her tree. It took a couple of pulls. If she'd been strong she'd have been able to do it with one arm.

"Mmm, mmf!" The woman's muffled cries came out like a prayer as her body left a scar in the leaf and bark litter.

Never leave a trace Aramanthis had been told by her dryad mother while she'd still been a tiny seed waiting to grow. Following the advice, she covered the scars in the detritus with a sweep of her foot.

The words were one of the few memories she had of her mother before being sent off to be reborn. She'd offered little advice to her children. There'd been plenty back then, so why devote time to just one? Aramanthis had no idea what had become of her sisters as they'd been scattered to the world. Aramanthis doubted her mother would have known she'd end up in Australia, carried by a human host until the conditions were right to bloom.

Aramanthis sat against her tree again to recover, as just dragging the human a few feet exhausted her. The hogtied woman began crying, whimpering into her gag.

"It sucks to be you," Aramathis said. "It sucks to be me even more."

She brushed the woman's greying hair from her eyes with a gentleness belying what she was about to do. On a sudden whimsy she leaned closer, but the woman whimpered and leaned away as far as she could.

The air wasn't cool enough to make the woman's breath frost, and Aramanthis wasn't warm blooded herself in the form she'd made for herself, but she could feel the warmth radiating from the woman's skin.

"I'm going to remove your gag," Aramanthis said softly. "Scream if you like. It's night and no one's around to hear, but I'll give you that chance if you want to take it."

The woman stared, her expression perplexed.

"Seriously," Aramanthis said. "You never know, someone at the main road might hear you, and I wouldn't care if they killed me to save you. It'd be nice to talk with you though, if you want to talk."

Without waiting for assent or acknowledgement, Aramanthis undid the gag and when it came away, she pulled a dirty rag from the woman's mouth. Surprisingly, the woman didn't scream. She just stared with a mixture of fear and astonishment.

"I'm Aramanthis. What's your name?"

The woman swallowed as if testing her mouth's newfound freedom. "Lucy."

Aramanthis smiled. She liked the name. "Do you believe in dryads, Lucy?"

Lucy shook her head slightly.

"And now you've met one. I'd never heard of them either until a dryad ensnared me with her perfume." She closed her eyes, smiling. "Fogged my head right up. I fell asleep against her tree's trunk in dappled sunlight on a warm spring day, and then I, well, I guess I died. To me it felt like I dreamed of whispered words, forests and trees, and for a long while I only knew the gentle sensation of rocking, like I was on a sailing ship. I was. Kind of. When the rocking ended I dreamed of water, a cool creek, and new life. I was reborn beside a fresh clean creek." She met Lucy's eyes. "I was born in England, and reborn in Australia. Can you tell from my accent?"

A little nervously by Aramanthis' guess, Lucy nodded.

"Are you from Canberra?"

Lucy nodded again, her hands struggling uselessly against the ropes as if hoping to free herself. Aramanthis smiled as she realised Lucy had a plan, just as she did. "Keep the crazy woman talking, hey Lucy? Maybe you'll find enough time to escape. Is that your intention?"

Lucy stiffened.

"Thought so. I'd do the same if I were you. Under other circumstances I'd enchant you with my perfume and you'd simply fall asleep, sparing you the fear and pain I'm about to inflict. Unfortunately you're going to feel… everything. I'm so sorry. I really am."

"What are you going to do?" Lucy asked, a quaver in her voice.

Aramanthis didn't want to think about the details. She'd heard the screams and felt the fear from all the victims Finn had bought her, and all because she couldn't spare the energy to lull them to sleep and make them dream as her mother had done for her.

"If I could, I'd use your lifeforce to nourish the plants around me," she said.

She rested the back of her head against her tree, feeling its strength. The tree wasn't affected by the poison, just her, yet there was so much silver in the ground it still hurt her.

"I'd be tempted to make you a deal if I had the strength. You could promise to find me someone to take your place, and I'd let you live. I'd even make you young again. Would you like that? Eternal youth, and protector to a dryad? You could be my gardener, and I'd be your eternal friend. You could start by taking a branch to the back of Finn's head. I'd happily trade him for you."

"Sure," Lucy said, clearly desperate enough to say anything to save herself. "I'll do that. I promise."

Aramanthis looked toward the big orange moon still rising from the horizon. It was a little smaller now. A little less orange. "You got kids Lucy?"

Lucy shook her head.

"I don't like to kill people with kids. It leaves a legacy that can have unintended consequences. People go looking for their loved ones. Having kids wouldn't have saved you, but it would have been worth saying you did."

Why was she rambling? She glanced at Lucy as she silently answered her own question. To put the inevitable off. She didn't want to hurt the woman. She didn't want to hurt anyone any more. Even humans. She knew their pain all too well.

She turned her head and caressed her tree's smooth white bark with her cheek, feeling the ache of silver in the ground through its roots. If she was honest with herself she'd admit she was dying. Slowly, but definitely.

Fresh lifeforce would delay the inevitable, but she wasn't sure how she'd escape if she couldn't remove the spikes. The path she could crack over time, and they'd probably replace it with un-poisoned concrete. The spikes were another matter.

Gently rubbing her cheek against the bark, the tree's solidity washed away the pain of silver for just a moment. Despite her denials and the hope they bought, she didn't see a way forward, at least not in this century.

Even if she did as Finn wanted, sooner or later there wouldn't be enough lifeforce to keep her alive, even if she took everything from the plants in the Gardens.

She had to make sure Lucy was Finn's last victim. The woman's sacrifice, at least, might grow into something good.

"Did you know we're immortal, Lucy? Dryads, I mean? We don't age, though we can be killed. We do take lives though. Not many, normally, but enough to ensure we're strong, and enough to keep the woods surrounding us strong." She closed her eyes. "Can you imagine a world where killing's not necessary? I'd like to live in that world."

"Please let me go," Lucy finally said. "I won't tell anyone."

"Words nobody's said before. Ever." Aramanthis said with more sullenness than she'd intended. "I'm sorry. That was callous."

She turned her attention back to the Gardens, her once beautiful abode now stung with drought and her own lack of care.

"Do you have any idea how many human skeletons reside below

the ground you're lying on?" She didn't wait for Lucy to answer. "Dozens."

Lucy closed her eyes and turned her face as far away as she could. When Aramanthis glanced down she found fresh tears silently streaking the woman's face. "You seem like a really nice person Lucy. Do you like plants?"

It took a little while, but Lucy eventually nodded. "I'd be lost without my flowers," she said.

"That's good. I think I like you a little more." Aramanthis gently placed her palm against her tree's biggest trunk and let her thoughts meld with its slowness.

Enraptured, she guided her tree's fine roots to break free of the soil and wrap around Lucy to the sound of a muffled cry, and then a scream. Lucy screamed again and again as the roots drew her down into the cool earth. Her screams became muffled, and then Aramanthis heard nothing but the quiet of the night.

She could still feel Lucy's fear and pain, and no doubt Lucy still screamed in her mind, but Aramanthis couldn't face sending her thoughts into the roots to check.

Sinking her mind deeper into her tree's heartwood instead, she guided the roots to properly cocoon Lucy as she drew out the woman's lifeforce.

In other circumstances she could survive on a single human's lifeforce for decades. Not now though. She had to make nectar.

Aramanthis didn't just take Lucy's energy though. She compressed the woman's thoughts, her dreams and her hopes, her very mind, and shrunk them down to a concentrated speck. Near dawn, when almost done, Aramanthis focused Lucy's very essence and lovingly reformed the woman's former body into something new and tiny and fresh.

Aramanthis barely had enough strength to finish her task as she moved everything that had once been Lucy through her tree. In moments her tree bloomed with a single flower, and as Aramanthis held out her hand a tiny seed the size of a grain of sand dropped from the heights to her palm.

"I'm sorry Lucy," she whispered to the seed. Her daughter. "Like my mother before me, I won't be there to guide you when you wake. All I can offer is a chance for revenge. Our revenge."

She leaned back, pressing her temporary body against her tree, and made her palm grow a leaf which twisted into a funnel-shaped cup.

She poured her body's lifeforce into the leaf cup then, using her own energy rather than Lucy's to make the nectar. Like syrup, it filled the leaf cup, and as the last of her strength dissipated she dropped Lucy's seed into it.

As her body hardened into wood she sent everything remaining of her consciousness into her tree.

Perhaps her tree would survive without her stewardship and keep her spirit safe. In a century or two, if she could find the strength to purge the silver from the ground and draw enough lifeforce from the Gardens, she could emerge anew.

For now she let what had recently been her body harden back to wood. In moments it dried out and cracked as if it were a carving, leaving only the nectar in it's cup.

"I name you Silver Rain, Silrain for short, for the moonlight falling upon us," Aramanthis whispered through the gentle breeze to her daughter, the seed which would become her first and possibly only child.

She wanted to give Silrain better advice than her own mother had offered.

"Finn, or whoever drinks the nectar holding you will grow thirsty and desperate for seclusion in the coming months. They'll shy away from people and carry you to fresh flowing water. Hopefully they'll find you a quiet, shady place that's difficult to get to, and even more difficult to find. There you can sprout and grow and be safe, perhaps for centuries, dear daughter."

"Protect your new garden, but not as I did. You don't need a gardener. Don't risk anyone trapping you."

With that, Aramanthis drifted into dreams where she was once again a seed, carried far from her mother to a new land where she would be reborn, just as Silrain would be.

When Finn returned he'd find what was left of her body, and with a little luck he'd drink her nectar himself along with the seed that had once been Lucy.

Afterward

Silver Rain on a Moonlight Night began with a slightly different premise - a man working at the Australian National Botanical Gardens as a labourer discovers the footpath he's laying is also trapping a dryad, with his boss as the bad guy.

The problem was, it started getting far too convoluted from there, largely due to the backstory I'd developed. It would have turned into a full-blown novel had I kept going with it.

I might revisit the idea if I get the time and perhaps create the bigger story, but not any time soon. I've already got too many novels to edit and/or write.

IN NEED OF ASSISTANCE

A SCIENCE FICTION SHORT STORY

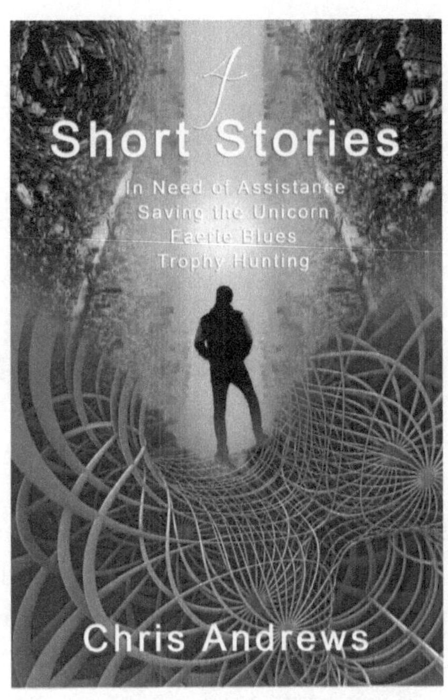

The seedship Antario burst out of hyperspace into the Rathor System, its hull bleeding atmosphere. Alarms rang and the ship shuddered. Jezz powered down the aft thrusters and shut off everything but life support and essential systems. The shuddering rapidly eased. He counted to ten, wiped perspiration from his brow and powered up the reverse thrusters. The ship rocked violently with an explosion, knocking the picture of his wife from the console. Power cut out and the bridge fell into total darkness.

He panicked for a moment, but emergency power engaged and the essential systems came back on. Jezz ran an analysis. The heart of the ship, its core, had cracked. Unless he found a way to slow Antario down, the Krael would vaporise him.

He shut off the core and rerouted power from the remaining fuel cells. The ship's lights dimmed and life support failed, but the reverse thrusters powered up again, this time without shuddering. "Thank God," he muttered.

Jezz opened communications. "Seedship Antario requesting permission to dock."

The translated response came through. "State your business and cargo, Antario."

The Krael didn't like visitors to Rathor. The quarantined planet supplied most of their bio-medical stocks.

Jezz touched the comm again. "There was a pirate attack on approach to Naporsicus II. I barely got away. I have a cargo of thirty-thousand drop pods, class one; basic Earth organisms."

"Again, state your business, Antario."

"Arrogant sods," he muttered. He hit the comm again. "My business is repairs and refuelling. Life support has failed and the core needs replacement. You're welcome to scan for confirmation."

The communication link went quiet. A drip of perspiration ran down Jezz's cheek. They could turn him away or even kill him and take the ship. No one would know. The Krael were cunning bastards though. He suspected they'd be considering how to acquire his terraforming cargo legitimately: a plethora of restricted lifeforms they could exploit.

"Seedship Antario, proceed to quarantine platform 3-QR. Coordinates will follow."

His console flashed with docking instructions. He wondered what they were planning; how they'd justify stealing his cargo. The cost of repairs, perhaps, with his signature sealing the deal.

It took two hours to get his limping wreck into orbit. Jezz double-checked his position – fifteen minutes to dock. Barely enough oxygen.

The planet before him was beautiful. He found the image of his deceased wife on the floor, picked it up and turned it toward the planet. "You always loved seeing a world from space."

He turned the image back toward himself, positioning it carefully on the console. "It took me a decade, but this one's for you, honey." He activated the ship's drop sequence. Three thousand pods released and curved toward Rathor's surface. Jezz disengaged the safeguards and rerouted all power to one of his forward thrusters. It blew, the shock rocking the ship. The lights momentarily dimmed.

The comm system lit up, but for the moment he ignored it while he rerouted power away from the blown thruster.

Just one injection would have saved her, if they'd had the money. He'd sold everything, and borrowed all he could, even begged, but it wasn't enough. And the Krael had the only cure, supplied from the biomeds grown on the world below.

"Bastards," he muttered at the comm. He opened communications and faked panic. "Seedship Antario requesting assistance! Please respond!" He cut the ship's communications and blew another thruster for effect. The ship began listing.

He wondered how long it would take them to figure it out, though he doubted his motivations would ever surface. Perhaps when they discovered he'd hijacked the ship and damaged it himself. Not that it mattered.

His monitors tracked the canisters falling through the atmosphere. They burst open, scattering bacteria, spores, algae and every other conceivable earth-type micro-organism to the winds, effectively seeding the planet with essential Earth life. On Rathor, the new organisms would raise oxygen levels, modify the climate, and eventually alter the entire ecosystem. The Krael would need centuries to repair the damage, if it were even possible.

Antario coasted on, only inertia keeping it in orbit now. Jezz closed his eyes and leaned back into his chair, smiling at the memories of his wife's lips on his. It wouldn't be long before they vaporised his ship now, he guessed. They'd figure it out soon.

Surprisingly, a second volley of canisters launched. He leaned back in his chair, his smile widening, at least for a few more seconds.

Afterward

In some ways, In Need of Assistance came about as a reaction to the many invasive plants and animals that have colonised Australia since European settlement.

That's hardly an earth-shattering premise, or even a premise at all, but it was the seed (boom, boom) of an idea which led to this story.

Fiction

Divine Prey: Normagaell Saga #1 - A Veil of Gods Novel.

Want to try before you buy? Read the first seven chapters for free - the first chapter is available on this page:

www.chrisandrews.me/divine-prey

The link to the remaining chapters is at the end.

Non-Fiction

Character and Structure: An Unholy Alliance

ABOUT THE AUTHOR

Chris Andrews is an author of science fiction, fantasy and horror.

Find him at - http://chrisandrews.me

Stay in Touch
Subscribe to Chris's Newsletter

facebook.com/chrisandrewsau
twitter.com/ChrisAndrewsAU
instagram.com/chrisandrews.me
amazon.com/author/chrisandrews